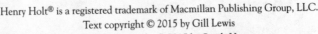

Henry Holt and Company, *Publishers since 1866*
175 Fifth Avenue, New York, NY 10010
mackids.com

Library of Congress Cataloging-in-Publication Data
Names: Lewis, Gill, author. | Horne, Sarah, 1979– illustrator.
Title: Scout and the sausage thief / Gill Lewis ; illustrations by Sarah Horne.
Description: First American edition. | New York : Henry Holt and Company,
2016. | Series: Puppy Academy | Summary: "Scout wants nothing more than
to be a police dog, just like her mom and dad. But when she fails her test,
Scout isn't sure she'll ever earn her badge until, that is, a sausage thief strikes.
It's up to Scout to catch the culprit and save the day" —Provided by publisher.
Identifiers: LCCN 2015042252 (print) | LCCN 2016021114 (ebook)
ISBN 9781627797948 (hardback) | ISBN 9781627798020 (trade paperback)
ISBN 9781627797955 (ebook)
Subjects: | CYAC: Mystery and detective stories. | Dogs—Fiction. |
Animals—Infancy—Fiction. | Robbers and outlaws—Fiction. | Working
dogs—Fiction. | BISAC: JUVENILE FICTION / Animals / Dogs. |
JUVENILE FICTION / Action & Adventure / General. |
JUVENILE FICTION / Humorous Stories.
Classification: LCC PZ7.L58537 Sco 2016 (print) | LCC PZ7.L58537 (ebook)
DDC [Fic]—dc23
LC record available at https://lccn.loc.gov/2015042252

Our books may be purchased in bulk for promotional, educational,
or business use. Please contact your local bookseller or the Macmillan
Corporate and Premium Sales Department at (800) 221-7945 ext. 5442
or by email at MacmillanSpecialMarkets@macmillan.com.

Originally published in the UK in 2015 by Oxford University Press
First American edition—2016

Printed in the United States of America by
LSC Communications, Harrisonburg, Virginia

ISBN 978-1-250-21761-5 (paper over board)

1 3 5 7 9 10 8 6 4 2

PUPPY ACADEMY

SCOUT
and the Sausage Thief

Gill Lewis

illustrations by Sarah Horne

 Henry Holt and Company ❧ New York

Welcome to Sausage Dreams Puppy Academy, where a team of plucky young pups are learning how to be all sorts of working dogs. Let's meet some of the students . . .

SCOUT

the smart one!

BREED: German Shepherd

SPECIAL SKILL:
Sniffing out
crime

STAR

the speedy one!

BREED: Border collie

SPECIAL SKILL:
Sensing danger

PIP

the friendly one!

BREED: Labrador retriever

SPECIAL SKILL: Ball games

MURPHY

the big one!

BREED: Leonberger

SPECIAL SKILL: Swimming

MAJOR BONES

One of the teachers at the
Sausage Dreams Puppy
Academy. Known for
being strict.

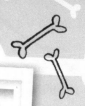

PROFESSOR OFFENBACH

Head of the Sausage
Dreams Puppy Academy.
She is a small dog with
A VERY LOUD VOICE!

1

Scout hid behind the stack of baked-bean cans and waited. The supermarket was busy with Saturday morning shoppers. She knew this was the moment when Frank Furter, the notorious sausage thief, would strike again. He could steal a salami from a sandwich or a hot dog from a hot-dog stand without ever being seen. No police dog had caught him in action yet.

No one knew just how Frank Furter stole the sausages. But Scout thought she knew. She'd worked it out and now she was ready. She looked up at the ceiling of the supermarket and waited for Frank's next move.

High above people's heads, one white ceiling tile slid slowly sideways. Frank's face appeared in the gap, spying down on the fresh-meat counter. Scout could see the bungee cord tied around his chest. She'd have to be quick on her feet to catch him.

Down came Frank.

2

"Gotcha!" shouted Scout.

She pounced, wrapping the string of sausages around and around him, tying him up in a big sausage knot.

Everyone cheered. Frank Furter had been caught at last, and Scout was their hero.

"Scout!"

"Scout!"

Scout woke up from her daydream.

"Come on, Scout," said her mom. "Finish your breakfast. You can't be late for school today."

"Do you think Frank Furter will ever be caught?" said Scout.

Scout's dad put down his paper. "He's very clever. No one has worked out just how he steals the sausages."

"But how do you know it's him?" asked Scout.

"Frank's pawprints are found all over the crime scenes," said Scout's dad. He shook his head. "Your mom and I have been working on this investigation for months. If we don't catch him before the weekend, the village sausage festival will have to be canceled."

"Canceled?" said Scout. "But it's

the most famous sausage festival in the world."

"I know," said Mom. "But unless Frank is caught, no one's sausages are safe. These are dark times. There hasn't been a case like this since Peppa Roni the Italian Spinoni hijacked Burt the Butcher's truck."

Scout frowned. "If anyone can catch Frank, you and Dad can."

Scout's mom sighed. "I hope so, Scout. I hope so."

Scout's mom and dad were well-known police dogs. They were loved by the villagers and feared by burglars. Until the recent spate of sausage robberies, there hadn't been a crime in Little Barking for three years.

"Frank trained to be a police dog with us when we were at Puppy Academy," said Scout's mom. "He had a thing about sausages even back then."

"Frank Furter was a police dog?!" said Scout. "But he should know not to break the law."

Scout's dad looked across at her. "There have been a few police dogs who have forgotten their vows."

Scout put her paw to her chest. "I vow to be honest, brave, and true, and to serve my fellow dogs and humans too."

"And above all else, be kind." Scout's mom smiled. "I'm sure you will make a great police dog one day."

Scout puffed out her chest in pride. She was a German shepherd.

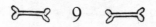

She wanted to be a police dog like her mom and dad. She wanted to catch burglars, find lost children, and keep everyone in Little Barking safe.

"You look sharp in your new collar," said Scout's dad.

"I have to look my best today," said Scout. "Our first test for our Care in the Community badge is to present ourselves to Major Bones."

Scout went to the Sausage Dreams Puppy Academy for working dogs, where she was training to become a police dog. There were all sorts of puppies at the academy. Some were training to be sheepdogs. Others were training for water rescue or mountain rescue. And others wanted to assist humans who were blind or hard of hearing. There were so many different jobs for the puppies to choose from.

"Don't forget your coat," said Scout's mom. "There's more rain forecast for today."

Scout's dad looked at the water pooling outside the kennel. "The river is rising and the duck brigade is on standby for any flooding. The new houses by the river are at risk if it keeps raining like this."

Scout put on her coat and looked at the row of badges she'd earned so far. She hoped she could add the Care in the Community badge by the end of the day.

Scout set off for the Puppy Academy. Despite the rain, she was feeling happy. She trotted through the main street of Little Barking. The village was busy with humans on their way to work and to school. Ahead, a crowd had gathered outside the butcher's shop. Scout pushed her way through to find out what the fuss was about.

Burt the Butcher was standing in the doorway, red-faced and shaking his fist in the air. The meat trays

in his shop window were sausage-less.

"The sausage thief has struck again!" shouted Burt.

There were gasps of horror from the crowd.

"The sausage festival will be canceled," wailed one woman.

Scout looked around at the shocked faces, but she knew it was too late to do anything. Frank Furter, the master cold-meats criminal, would be far away already.

Scout set off again. She was weaving her way in and out of parents with strollers and children on their way to school when she stumbled upon something on the ground.

It was a threadbare teddy with a missing eye and a bandage on its paw. It lay in a puddle with a big, muddy footprint on its tummy.

It looked sad and lonely. Scout sniffed it. Beneath the mud and water, it smelled of strawberry shampoo and cheese-and-pickle sandwiches.

Scout knew that someone loved this teddy. She looked around to see if anyone was looking for it, but everyone was hurrying to get out of the rain.

A human child must have dropped this on the way to school, she thought. Maybe she should take it to the school, but she knew that would make her late for her test. Maybe she should leave it here. Whoever lost it might find it on the way home.

Scout sat the teddy on a bench and walked on, but deep inside she just knew that someone wanted this teddy back. She couldn't leave it. Scout turned around, picked up the teddy, and trotted to the school. She followed the long line of children to the school gates. A small girl smelling of strawberry shampoo was sobbing in her mother's arms.

Scout trotted up and pushed the teddy into the girl's hands.

"Eddie!" cried the girl. "You're alive!" She hugged her teddy tight against her.

"Clever pup," said the girl's mother, patting Scout on the head. "However did you find him?"

Scout wanted to tell her where she'd found the teddy, but she knew humans didn't understand woofs and barks, so she just wagged her tail instead.

The girl reached into her bag and offered Scout a cheese-and-pickle sandwich, but at that moment the school bell rang. It was time for Scout to go to school too.

She turned and ran. She couldn't be late. She had to make it to Puppy Academy on time.

2

Scout ran out of the school gates. If
she took the shortcut through the
park, she might be able to get to the
academy in time for the first test.
She squeezed through the hedge,
the brambles catching and sticking
in her fur. Her feet raced across
the field, mud flying up from her
paws.

As she ran through the academy

gates, she could see her class lining up in the hall. She rushed in to join them, mud and rain dripping from her coat, brambles stuck in her fur and collar.

"Where have you been?" whispered Lulu.

"We've been waiting for you," said Murphy.

"You're late!" Major Bones glared at her. Major Bones was one of the teachers at Puppy Academy, and he was known for being strict.

"I'm sorry," panted Scout, "but—"

"No buts," woofed Major Bones. He looked Scout up and down. "You look like you've been dragged through a hedge!"

"I have—" began Scout.

Major Bones tutted. "You do realize good presentation is one of your Care in the Community tests today?"

"Yes," said Scout. "I—"

"No excuses, Scout. I can't pass

you looking like that. Now go and
get yourself cleaned up and join us
for the crosswalk test."

Scout ran off, her tail between
her legs. She tried to brush the mud
from her fur, but it stuck in thick
clumps and she couldn't remove it
all. It would have to do.

She rejoined Major Bones and the other pups in the hall. Rain hammered on the roof above.

"Normally, we would do the crosswalk test outside," said Major Bones, "but as it's raining, we'll take the test in the hall today."

The pups all looked at the crosswalk chalked on the ground. Scout felt her legs shaking. She wasn't off to a good start. She had to do well in this next test. She *had* to.

"We're very lucky to have Mrs. Chubbs, the pet shop owner, here today," woofed Major Bones. "She has volunteered to be our human in need, and she has generously donated a large bag of Crunchie Munchies for you all to share after the test."

All the puppies barked and wagged their tails. Crunchie Munchies were everyone's favorite treats.

"Today I will be testing you on how to help someone across a busy street," woofed Major Bones.

Mrs. Chubbs shuffled onto the training ground. She walked slowly with the help of a cane. She gave all the puppies a little wave. Scout sat up straight, her feet together and her ears pricked up. She wanted Major Bones to know she could do this.

"Let's have Murphy first," said Major Bones.

Murphy trotted forward. He took Mrs. Chubbs gently by the sleeve, looked left and right and left again, and guided her over the crossing.

"Well done, well done," said Major Bones. "I hope everyone was watching Murphy, because that's how to do it."

Murphy trotted back to the line of puppies, his head held high.

"Now, let's have Scout," woofed Major Bones.

Scout felt nervous. She didn't want to mess this up. Her muscles were in tight knots.

She grabbed Mrs. Chubbs.

"Ow! Oooh! My arm!" cried Mrs. Chubbs.

Scout let go. In her rush, she'd grabbed Mrs. Chubbs's arm, not her sleeve. Scout backed away, knocking Mrs. Chubbs's cane from under her.

"SCOUT! BE CAREFUL!" bellowed Major Bones as Mrs. Chubbs clattered to the ground.

Scout looked between Mrs. Chubbs and Major Bones. "I didn't mean to! I'm sorry."

Major Bones helped Mrs. Chubbs to her feet. He shook his head. "I don't know what's gotten into you today, Scout. I think you'd better come and see me in my office. I don't think you're up to taking the rest of your Care in the Community tests today."

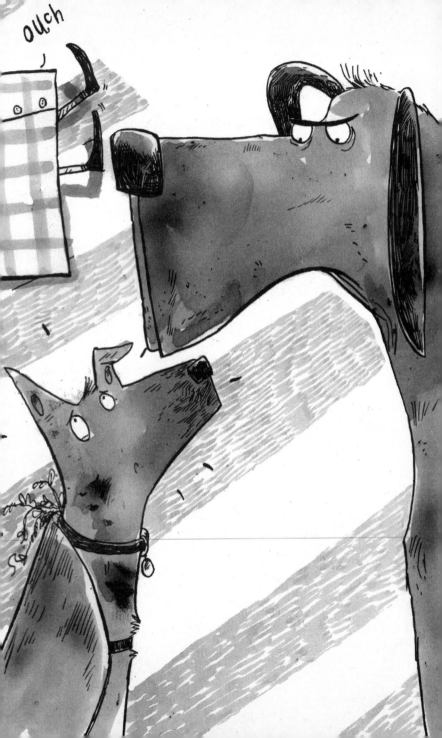

3

Scout stood and waited for Major Bones in his office. There were piles of papers everywhere, boxes stuffed with books, and drawers bursting with pens and pencils. There were agility hoops and jumps packed against the back wall. Scout couldn't even see the surface of the desk.

"Ah, Scout," said Major Bones, coming into the room. "Sit down, sit down."

Scout looked around but couldn't see a spare seat beneath the mess.

Major Bones sat down in his chair. "So, Scout. I'm here to listen. In your own words, tell me what went wrong today."

"Well," said Scout, "I—"

RING! RING! RING! RING!

"Excuse me," said Major Bones. "I'd better take that call."

Major Bones searched under boxes and piles of paper.

"Now, where did I put that phone?" he muttered.

He searched and searched until the phone stopped ringing.

"Never mind," said Major Bones. "Where were we . . . Ah, yes! Well, Scout. I'm sorry to say that I won't be able to award you the Care in the Community badge today. You haven't passed the presentation test or the crosswalk test." He frowned. "Really, Scout, I'm not sure you even want this badge. Take a good look at yourself. You've come to school plastered in mud and brambles."

Scout stared down at the floor. She hadn't had a chance to tell her side of the story. "I'm sorry," she whimpered.

"Don't worry, young pup." Major Bones sighed. "No harm done. Mrs. Chubbs is fine after her fall. You'll just have to try a little harder next time." He glanced at the mud and brambles in her coat. "Maybe avoid the park next time too."

Scout nodded, but she had wanted to pass the test with her friends. She didn't want her mom and dad to know she'd failed.

"In the meantime," said Major Bones, "I'd like you to take the bag of Crunchie Munchies to the food shed. The lock has broken, so I'll put you on guard duty until the others have finished their tests."

Scout helped Major Bones carry the bag across the yard. The rain had stopped, but the clouds looked dark and swollen with more rain. Major Bones placed the Crunchie Munchies in the food shed and closed the door.

"Right, Scout," he said. "Your job is to guard the Crunchie Munchies. Can you do that for me?"

Scout nodded. She watched Major Bones walk away to join the other pups in the class and continue the tests without her.

Scout shivered. A cold wind was blowing, finding its way through her thick fur to her skin. She wanted to find shelter, but she had to guard the food shed.

While she waited, Scout looked out across the academy. At the bottom of the hill she could see the new housing development where the river-meadows used to be. The river looked brown and swollen and had risen to the tops of the banks.

"Hey, Scout! It's break time. Are you okay?"

Scout looked up to see Gwen, Murphy, Scruff, and Lulu walking over to her.

"I'm okay," she said, trying to sound cheerful. "How are the tests?"

"They're all right," said Gwen. "We had to find a lost child and then rescue a cat from a tree."

Scout put her head on her paws. She wished she could have done the tests with them. She was missing all the fun.

"Come and play with us," woofed Gwen. "We've got a break until lunchtime."

Scout shook her head. "I have to guard the food shed."

"It's not as if anyone's going to steal the treats," Gwen said.

"You never know," said Scruff. "Frank Furter hasn't been caught yet."

"But he goes after sausages, not Crunchie Munchies," said Lulu.

"How do you think he steals the sausages?" said Murphy.

"Invisibility cape," said Gwen. "That's what my brother says."

"My dad thinks he's invented a sausage magnet," woofed Scruff.

"No one knows," said Scout. "That's the thing. No one knows how he does it."

"So you're not coming to play?" said Gwen.

Scout shook her head. Her duty was to guard the food shed. Even if she couldn't be a police dog, she could act like one.

"See you later then," said Murphy.

Scout stayed by the food shed.
She didn't move. Her stomach
rumbled all through lunchtime and
into the afternoon. She watched
her classmates do the rest of their
Care in the Community tests. She
watched them picking up litter

and practicing to keep the peace
at the sausage festival. Last year
the festival had turned ugly when
Verity's Vegan Sausages scooped first
prize over Burt's Black Pudding.

Scout heard Professor Offenbach
call everyone together in the hall.
Professor Offenbach was the head
of the Sausage Dreams Puppy
Academy. She was a small dog with
a big voice that boomed out across
the academy.

Scout sat and waited by the food
shed and listened.

**"WELCOME, PUPS, TO OUR
FRIDAY AWARD CEREMONY. IT'S**

BEEN ANOTHER BUSY WEEK AT THE ACADEMY. TODAY WE HAVE BADGES TO GIVE OUT FOR CARE IN THE COMMUNITY. THIS IS A VERY SPECIAL BADGE INDEED. I'D LIKE TO CALL MURPHY, GWEN, LULU, AND SCRUFF UP TO THE GIANT SAUSAGE PODIUM TO RECEIVE THEIR AWARDS."

Scout wished she could be up at the podium too. What would her mom and dad say when they found out she was the only pup in her class not to receive the badge?

"AND," woofed Professor

Offenbach, **"WE CAN NOW CELEBRATE WITH MRS. CHUBBS'S CRUNCHIE MUNCHIES!"**

All the pups cheered, and Scout watched them racing toward her and the food shed. She wasn't sure she felt like Crunchie Munchies anymore.

"Hi, Scout," said Gwen.

"Well done for getting

your Care in the Community badge," said Scout. She tried her best to smile.

"Now then," said Major Bones. "Who would like a Crunchie Munchie?"

The other pups all put their paws in the air.

Major Bones opened the food shed and went inside.

He didn't come out with the Crunchie Munchies. He came out with a frown on his face instead. "Scout," he said, "have you been here all this time?"

"I haven't moved a muscle, sir," said Scout.

"Has anyone been in the food shed?"

"No," said Scout.

Major Bones walked all the way around the food shed and bent down to look Scout in the eye. "Are you sure?"

"Yes," said Scout. "No one else has been here."

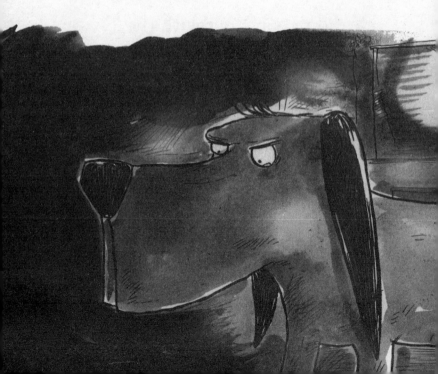

Major Bones looked at the crowd. "We have a problem," he said.

The puppies all glanced at one another.

Major Bones pulled himself up to his full height. "The problem is, the Crunchie Munchies . . . are missing!"

4

"Impossible," said Scout. "I haven't seen anyone carry the bag away."

"It isn't the bag that is missing," said Major Bones. "The bag is still there. The Crunchie Munchies have disappeared. Someone has eaten them all."

The pups fell silent. Scout could feel their eyes on her.

"How could that happen?" Scout piped up. "I was here the whole time."

Lulu frowned. "No wonder you wanted to stay by the food shed. You wanted to eat the Crunchie Munchies all by yourself."

"No!" said Scout.

Murphy pointed his paw at her. "Maybe you were jealous of us, so you ate them because you didn't want us to have them too."

"That's not true!" said Scout. How could they think that about her?

Scruff scrunched up her nose. "Well, tell us where they are."

"I . . . I . . . can't," said Scout, looking at them all. She put her head in the shed to see the empty bag on the floor. "They've just disappeared."

"Disappeared in your tummy, you mean," said Gwen. "We were looking forward to those treats. We deserved them, not you."

"Ahem," said Major Bones. "Let's not jump to conclusions. Let's think about this logically. So, the Crunchie Munchies were placed in the shed."

"Correct," said Scout.

"And you guarded the door," said Major Bones.

"Correct," said Scout.

"You saw no one enter or leave the building?"

"No one," said Scout.

Major Bones walked all the way around the shed. "There are no other doors or windows to the shed."

Scout followed him. "No."

"Hmm," said Major Bones. "You see, Scout, you are the only pup to have been near the Crunchie Munchies. I'm afraid it's beginning to look very suspicious."

"I didn't eat them," said Scout. "Maybe it was Frank Furter. No one has caught him stealing yet."

Gwen narrowed her eyes. "But he only steals sausages."

"Admit it, Scout," whispered Lulu. "You're the thief."

"Thief! Thief! Thief!" Angry puppy faces closed in on Scout.

"NO!" wailed Scout, looking wildly around.

"That's enough," Major Bones
said to the pups. He turned to Scout.
"I'm afraid you must come with me.
I will need to see you in my office
with Professor Offenbach while we
decide just what to do."

Scout stood in Major Bones's office
for the second time that day. She
stared at her paws. She felt like a
criminal. She felt guilty even though
she knew she hadn't done anything
wrong.

"Hmmm," said Major Bones,
again. "This is a difficult situation."

"VERY DIFFICULT," boomed
Professor Offenbach.

"Scout," said Major Bones, "We're here to listen to your side of the story. Please tell us, in your own words, what happened today with the Crunchie Munchies."

RING! RING! RING! RING!

"Excuse me," said Major Bones. "I should take that call."

Major Bones lifted up piles of
paper and boxes. "Now, where did I
put that phone?" he muttered.

Professor Offenbach rolled her
eyes.

Major Bones searched until the
phone stopped ringing.

"Never mind," he said. "Now, where were we? Ah, yes. You see, Scout, we're in a very difficult situation. You were put in charge of the Crunchie Munchies, and now they have gone missing. I'm afraid the paw of blame seems to be pointing at you."

Scout stared at them wide-eyed. She couldn't believe what they were suggesting. They hadn't even heard her side of the story.

"OF COURSE, WE'RE NOT BLAMING YOU AT THIS STAGE," barked Professor Offenbach, **"BUT UNTIL WE FIND OUT EXACTLY**

WHAT HAPPENED, WE WILL
HAVE TO ASK YOU TO LEAVE
THE ACADEMY."

"Leave?" said Scout.

"I'm afraid so," said Major Bones.
"We need to find out what happened
to the missing Crunchie Munchies.
We don't know who took them, but

we will find out. We can't have liars and thieves within the academy."

"I didn't do it," blurted Scout. "You do believe me, don't you?" She searched both their faces. "Don't you?"

Major Bones fiddled with some papers on his desk.

Professor Offenbach put a paw on her shoulder and looked down at her with sad eyes.

Scout didn't want to stay a minute longer. She turned away from them both and ran.

5

Leave the academy? It was an impossible thought. Now she would never be a police dog—ever.

The other pups were waiting for her outside.

"Why did you do it?" Murphy said. "We would have shared our treats with you."

"I didn't. Please believe me," pleaded Scout. "I didn't."

"You were the only one there," said Scruff. "Who else could it have been?"

Scout looked from pup to pup. They thought she was a liar and a thief, and there was nothing she could do about it. Her mom and dad would probably think so too. Scout had never felt so utterly helpless and alone.

A sharp wind ruffled Scout's fur. Dark clouds marched across the sky and big drops of rain began to fall, *plip-plop-plip-plop*, faster and faster. The gutters ran with water. Lightning flashed and thunder rumbled overhead. The rain poured through Scout's thick coat and dripped off the end of her nose, but the coldness she felt was deep down inside. She had been asked to leave the academy. It was all over. Her dreams were shattered. Everything had gone horribly, horribly wrong.

Scout ran out of the grounds and into the storm. It was hard to see through the driving rain, but Scout ran and ran. She didn't know where to go. She couldn't face going home, so she ran away from the village, down to the new houses where the river-meadows used to be.

The road was blocked. The river had finally burst its banks, and brown water was swirling into gardens and flowing through doorways. Scout could see her mom and dad helping people onto dry land.

Scout didn't want to tell her parents why she'd had to leave the academy, so she turned and ran the other way.

She ran past the hastily abandoned bungalows, which older humans liked to live in. Maybe she could hide away in one of them for a while. But the river was steadily rising, and it would soon cut her off. Plastic chairs and tables were already floating in people's gardens. Despite her own misery, she was glad the older folks had been taken to safety.

Scout stopped in her tracks. Not everyone had made it to safety!

Someone had been left behind.

A stooped figure in a long hooded raincoat was struggling out of a garden shed. Maybe he hadn't heard the rescuers. Floodwater sloshed over his boots as he headed for his bungalow.

"Hello," woofed Scout. But the old man didn't seem to hear her above the rain.

Scout watched him wade in through the front door. She knew he wouldn't be safe in his bungalow. She had to get him out of there. She had to.

She paddled through the water to the front door.

"Hello," she woofed. "Hello!"

A sausage floated past her through the open door. Scout stared at it as it bobbed along to join the river.

She walked in and pushed open another door to the kitchen. The old man was there with his back to her. He was holding a sausage and reaching into the fridge for a bottle of ketchup.

There was something odd about the man, she thought. It wasn't so much the way he squeezed ketchup all over his sausage. It was the way a long tail was sticking out from the bottom of his raincoat.

"Frank Furter!" exclaimed Scout.

Frank spun around and glared at her, ketchup all over his paws.

"I've caught you red-pawed!" said Scout. "So this is how you've been stealing the sausages. You've been pretending to be a human!"

"Pesky pup!" said Frank, grabbing his bag of sausages. "I'm out of here."

"Not so fast!"

"Frank Furter, we arrest you in the name of the paw!"

Scout turned around to the voices she recognized.

"Mom! Dad!"

She watched while they put paw-cuffs on Frank.

"How did you know I was here?" said Scout.

"Major Bones came to tell us you'd been asked to leave the academy," said Scout's mom.

"Oh!" said Scout. She looked down at the water swirling in the kitchen.

"We saw you heading this way, so we came to look for you."

"You think I stole the Crunchie Munchies too, don't you?" said Scout.

Scout's dad put his big paw around her. "Of course we don't," he said. "We know you could never do a thing like that. We came to find you because we knew you'd be upset."

"You believe me?" said Scout.

Scout's mom smiled. "Of course we do. We know you're honest, brave, and true."

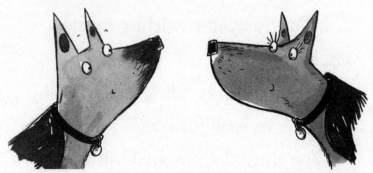

It felt as if a heavy weight had been lifted from Scout's chest.

"Thank you," she said. "But it still doesn't solve the mystery of the missing Crunchie Munchies."

"No," said her dad. "But you've solved the mystery of the sausage thief."

Frank glared at Scout. "If it hadn't been for your do-gooding ways, I'd have been long gone by now."

Scout's mom said, "Thanks to you, Scout, the Little Barking Sausage Festival can go ahead again this year."

GRRRRR...

The river had risen even higher.

"Come on," said Scout's dad.
"We'll need to dog-paddle out of
here—and quickly!"

As Scout followed her parents
and Frank through the front gate,
she heard cries for help coming from
the garden shed.

"HELP US, HEEEELP! HELP! OVER HERE! SAVE US!"

"Stop!" Scout shouted to her mom and dad. But they were ahead of her, carrying Frank through the water, and they did not hear her.

"HELP US, HEEEELP! HELP!"

Without thinking, Scout turned

and started swimming toward the shed. She pushed her way through the door. In the corner, Scout could see a rusty bucket swirling around and around in the dirty water. The bucket seemed to be sinking deeper and deeper.

"HELP US, HEEEELP! HELP!"

The cries were coming from inside the bucket.

A family of field mice—a mom and a dad, aunties and uncles, grandma and granddad, and lots of tiny mouselings—were clinging to the rim.

they called.

Scout grabbed the bucket with her teeth and pulled it from the shed. She swam and swam, dragging the mouse-filled bucket to dry ground.

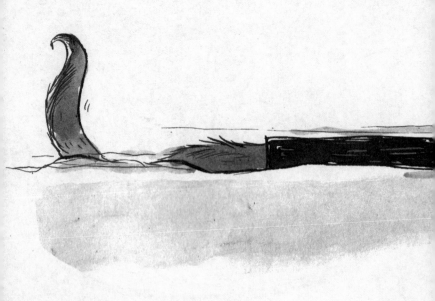

"THANK YOU FOR SAVING US," squeaked the field mice. "WE THOUGHT WE WERE DONE FOR."

Scout looked in at them. Her eyes opened wide, wide, wide . . . because the field mice were not the only things Scout could see in the bucket.

6

"The missing Crunchie Munchies!" said Major Bones, picking up a soggy Crunchie Munchie from the bottom of the bucket.

"You see, I didn't take them," blurted Scout. "The field mice said they carried them out from the food shed through a small crack in the floor."

"THIS CHANGES EVERYTHING," said Professor Offenbach.

Scout's mom looked long and hard at Major Bones and Professor Offenbach. "I do hope the academy remembers that everyone is innocent until proven guilty."

"Of course, of course," blustered

Major Bones. "Well, at least we've found the guilty culprits. It seems more than one thief has been caught today."

The field mice clung to one another and shivered with cold.

Major Bones bent down to get a closer look at them. "What were you thinking by stealing the pups' hard-earned treats? Explain yourselves."

RING! RING! RING! RING!

"Excuse me," said Major Bones, "I'd better take that call." Major Bones looked under the blanket in his dog bed. "Now, where did I put that phone?" he muttered.

He searched and searched until the phone stopped ringing.

"Never mind," said Major Bones. "Where were we . . . Ah, yes! Mice! You have been caught stealing from the academy. Scout's mom and dad will take you away and lock you up for a very, very long time."

"Wait!" said Scout. "You haven't listened to them. You haven't heard their side of the story."

"Haven't I?" said Major Bones, frowning.

"No," said Scout. "Shh! Let's listen."

The mother field mouse held her tail in her paws and looked up at Major Bones. "WE DIDN'T KNOW THE CRUNCHIE MUNCHIES WERE FOR THE PUPPIES," she said.

"WE WERE SO HUNGRY, YOU SEE. WE USED TO LIVE ON THE RIVER-MEADOW AND EAT THE WILD GRASSES AND FRUITS AND SEEDS. BUT SINCE THE HUMANS BUILT THEIR HOUSES, WE'VE HAD NOWHERE TO LIVE AND NOTHING TO EAT."

Major Bones sat down in his chair and rubbed his head. "Oh dear," he said. "I see. You should have asked, and we would have given you the Crunchie Munchies."

"WE JUST WANT OUR MEADOWS BACK," said the field mouse.

Major Bones frowned. "Oh dear, oh dear," he said. "That's not so easy. What should we do?"

Scout looked around Major Bones's office, at the piles of paper

and the pens scattered on the desk
and the overflowing wastebasket.

"Why don't the mice stay here
and tidy up your office in exchange
for Crunchie Munchies, until we
can find them a new field of their
own?" said Scout.

"Well," said Major Bones,
"I suppose my office could be
straightened up a bit."

The mice cheered squeaky cheers.
Scout looked up to see her mom
and dad beaming at her.

"WELCOME, PUPS, AGAIN."
Professor Offenbach had called all
the pups back into the hall.

"BEFORE WE GO HOME
TODAY, WE HAVE AN EXTRA
CELEBRATION. WE HAVE A VERY
BRAVE PUP AMONG US. PLEASE
WELCOME SCOUT TO THE
GIANT SAUSAGE PODIUM. NOT
ONLY HAS SCOUT HELPED TO

CATCH A NOTORIOUS CRIMINAL,
BUT, MORE IMPORTANT, TODAY
SCOUT HAS SHOWN US WHAT
CARE IN THE COMMUNITY IS
ALL ABOUT. SCOUT HAS SHOWN
US THAT WE MUST TAKE TIME
TO LISTEN TO ONE ANOTHER
AND UNDERSTAND OTHERS'
NEEDS SO THAT WE CAN ALL
LIVE ALONGSIDE EACH OTHER.
PLEASE ALL WAG YOUR TAILS
FOR SCOUT FOR GAINING HER
CARE IN THE COMMUNITY
BADGE."

All the pups wagged their tails and barked. Then they followed Scout to

Major Bones's office to meet the field mice and see how they were doing.

During the ceremony, the mice had worked quickly to tidy up all the papers and put the pens and pencils neatly in the pencil holders. Major Bones's office looked like a different place.

"I'm sorry I didn't believe you, Scout," said Gwen, hanging her head low.

"Me too," said Lulu.

"I wouldn't lie to you," said Scout.

"I know," said Scruff. "We should have trusted you. We were looking forward to the Crunchie Munchies so much and were sad to find them missing. It seemed easy to blame you."

"Can you forgive us?" said Murphy.

"Of course." Scout smiled. "It's a shame we never did get any Crunchie Munchies, though!"

RING! RING! RING! RING!

"Excuse me," said Major Bones, "I'd better take that call."

"HERE YOU ARE," said a field mouse,
handing Major Bones the phone.
"Oh, well done!" cried Major
Bones. "My phone! You found it!"

Major Bones held the phone to his ear. "Yes? Major Bones here. . . . Really? You've been trying to get hold of me all day? I see. . . . Did she? This morning, you say? Well, I never!" He glanced across at Scout several times. "I see. . . . Yes, I see. . . . Well, that's good to know. . . . Thank you. . . . Thank you. . . . I'll tell the pups the good news."

The pups all waited to hear what Major Bones had to say.

"Well," he said. "That was Bernie, the head teacher's dog at the primary school. It seems that I owe Scout another apology. The reason she was late today was because she was returning a lost teddy bear to a child. The girl's mother is sending a big bag of Crunchie Munchies to the academy as a thank-you. Scout really has earned her Care in the Community badge today."

Scout barked. "Crunchie Munchies all around, everyone!"

Scout trotted along with her mom
and dad to the sausage festival.

"Well," said Dad, "Frank is well
and truly behind bars, and the Little
Barking Sausage Festival is safe for
another year."

"So," said Scout's mom, "do you still want to be a police dog?"

"More than ever," woofed Scout.

"Come on," said Scout's dad. "After all that police work, I'm hungry. Anyone want a sausage?"

Scout stared at the rows upon rows of different sausages: pork and apple, beef and onion, venison and red currant, bratwursts, chipolatas, chorizos, Cumberland swirls . . . so many to choose from.

"Well . . . ?" said Dad.

"I'll have a bowl of water, please." Scout sighed. "I think I've just about had enough of sausages until next year."

Meet Leo, a real-life police tracker dog!

Name
Leo

Age
6

Occupation
Police tracker dog

Likes
Walks in the woods, tug-of-war

Hates
Bath time!

Tracked both the driver AND the passenger responsible for a jewel theft—and then found the loot as well!

Police Dog Facts

The first time dogs were used by the police is believed to be 1888, when two bloodhounds helped to track a criminal.

DID YOU KNOW?

Police dogs belong to K-9 (which stands for "canine") units in the United States.

German shepherds were first used as police dogs in London in 1948.

DID YOU KNOW?

Police dogs normally work for about eight to nine years.

Dogs and their handlers have to pass a test every year to make sure they are good enough to continue working for the police.

DID YOU KNOW?

When they retire, police dogs often go to live with their handler as a pet.

About Zak and his owner, Gill Lewis

I'm ZAK, a German shepherd just like Scout. I was GILL LEWIS's first dog. When she was fourteen, her wish to have a dog of her own came true and she got me. I like to think we got each other. I used to walk with her some of the way to school and meet her at the garden gate on her way home.

Some people think German shepherds are a bit fierce, but I was a big softy. I liked helping people too. I ran alongside GILL's bike when she did her paper route. I even carried some of the papers—until people complained of dog slobber on their Sunday news. Like Scout, I was only trying to help. . . .

Ready for big
adventure?

STAR

Want to know about
real-life working dogs?

No sheep
were harmed in
the making of
this book.

Henry Holt and Company, *Publishers since 1866*
175 Fifth Avenue, New York, NY 10010
mackids.com

Henry Holt® is a registered trademark of Macmillan Publishing Group, LLC.
Text copyright © 2015 by Gill Lewis
Illustrations copyright © 2015 by Sarah Horne
All rights reserved.

Library of Congress Cataloging-in-Publication Data
Names: Lewis, Gill, author. | Horne, Sarah, illustrator.
Title: Star on Stormy Mountain / Gill Lewis ; illustrations by Sarah Horne.
Description: First American edition. | New York : Henry Holt and
Company, 2016. | Series: Puppy Academy | Summary: "Everyone says
Star is much too fast to be a sheepdog, but when your mom is a sheepdog
champion, what else can you be? When a lamb goes missing on a field trip
to Stormy Mountain, Star races up to find it. But she soon discovers that the
lamb isn't the only one who needs her help" —Provided by publisher.
Identifiers: LCCN 2015042695 (print) | LCCN 2016021395 (ebook) |
ISBN 9781627797962 (hardback) | ISBN 9781627798037 (trade
paperback) | ISBN 9781627797979 (Ebook)
Subjects: | CYAC: Dogs—Fiction. | Animals—Infancy—Fiction. |
Sheep—Fiction. | Rescues—Fiction. | Working dogs—Fiction. | BISAC:
JUVENILE FICTION / Animals / Dogs. | JUVENILE FICTION / Action &
Adventure / General. | JUVENILE FICTION / Humorous Stories.
Classification: LCC PZ7.L58537 St 2016 (print) | LCC PZ7.L58537
(ebook) | DDC [Fic]—dc23
LC record available at https://lccn.loc.gov/2015042695

Our books may be purchased in bulk for promotional, educational,
or business use. Please contact your local bookseller or the Macmillan
Corporate and Premium Sales Department at (800) 221-7945 ext. 5442
or by email at MacmillanSpecialMarkets@macmillan.com.

Originally published in the UK in 2015 by Oxford University Press
First American edition—2016

Printed in the United States of America by
LSC Communications, Harrisonburg, Virginia

ISBN 978-1-250-21761-5 (paper over board)

1 3 5 7 9 10 8 6 4 2

PUPPY ACADEMY

STAR
on Stormy Mountain

Gill Lewis

illustrations by Sarah Horne

Henry Holt and Company ❖ New York

1

The collie pups—Star, Gwen, Nevis, and Shep—pushed their way to the front of the crowd gathered at the bottom of the hill. A hushed silence fell across the dogs and humans who were watching. It was the final round of the National Sheepdog Trials, and it looked like Bleak Tarn, the old, gnarled collie and five-time champion, would win again.

But there was one dog remaining—
one dog who still had to run the
course.

Gwen nudged Star with her paw.
"Look—here comes your mom."

The pups watched Star's mom,
Lillabelle of Langdale Pike, trot
alongside her shepherd. The black-
and-white collie waited at the starting
line for the signal, and then she

was off. She raced up the hillside in a long curve toward the small flock of sheep grazing in the far field. She leaped the low wall and came up behind the sheep, slowing down as she did so. She knew that if she ran in too fast, she would scare them and they would scatter. The sheep saw her and drew together. Lillabelle kept her head low and crept closer to them, and the small flock set off steadily down the hillside toward the crowd.

"That was perfect!" said Nevis.

"If the rest of the trial goes this well, your mom might win," said Shep.

Lillabelle guided the sheep through narrow gates, then drove them into a circle marked on the ground. Next, she had to single out the ewe with the green spot painted on her back. She circled the sheep, keeping them in a tight group, and when she saw the ewe on the outside of the flock, she swiftly trotted in and herded it away.

The crowd held their breath.

Maybe Lillabelle's performance was good enough to beat Bleak Tarn, but there was one last part of the trial to complete. It was the most difficult part of all. Lillabelle had to herd the sheep into the square pen and shut the gate. It wouldn't be easy. The sheep were getting bored and restless. They wanted to be back out on the hillside with the other flocks.

Lillabelle kept them calm. If she charged in now, all would be lost. She tried to forget the crowd watching her. She also tried to forget Bleak Tarn, who would be willing her to fail.

Keeping her belly low to the
ground, she crept forward. The
sheep bunched together more
tightly, looking for an escape route
to the hillside. But Lillabelle kept
them moving, and before they knew
it, the sheep had followed one
another into the pen. The shepherd

swung the gate shut, and the crowd
exploded with applause.

She had done it. Bleak Tarn had
been beaten at last.

There was a new winner now.

A new champion.

Lillabelle of Langdale Pike had
won the National Sheepdog Trials.

 7

Gwen turned to Star. "Your mom is awesome," she said.

"The best!" said Shep.

"My dad said she would win," said Nevis.

Star puffed out her chest in pride. Her mom was a champion sheepdog. Everyone said Star would be a champion too. Star hoped so. She hoped one day she would win the National Sheepdog Trials and make her mom proud.

Star was looking forward to tomorrow. Tomorrow was the beginning of the pups' sheepdog training, and Star couldn't wait.

The next morning, Star, Gwen, Nevis, and Shep gathered in the classroom.

"Right," said Major Bones. "It's time to get started on your basic sheepherding skills. We'll go out to the field and see if Hilda and Mabel are ready for us."

The four collie pups followed Major Bones outside. Major Bones

was a teacher at the Sausage Dreams
Puppy Academy for Working Dogs.
There were all sorts of puppies at the
Puppy Academy. There were pups who
were training to be guide dogs, pups
who wanted to be hearing dogs (to
help people who are deaf), and pups
who wanted to be water-rescue dogs.
But Star wanted to be a sheepdog

like her mom. She was a border collie, after all, and border collies had sheepherding in their blood.

Hilda and Mabel, the academy sheep, weren't in the field. They were in the barn, sitting on hay bales, chitchatting and knitting woolen blankets for dogs in rescue shelters.

"Ooh, hello, my dears," Hilda bleated, seeing the collie pups.

"Hello," baa-ed Mabel.

Hilda put her knitting down. "Well, if it isn't little Gwen, Shep, Nevis, and Star," she bleated. She gave Star a little wink. "We're expecting great things from you."

"Great things," baa-ed Mabel in agreement.

Star smiled to herself. She imagined winning the National Sheepdog Trials: Star of Langdale Pike, the new champion.

"No need for idle talk," barked Major Bones. "Let's get started."

"Right-ho, right-ho," bleated Hilda. "Just give me time. My legs don't move as fast as they used to."

"Not as fast," baa-ed Mabel.

They climbed down from their hay bales and hobbled outside into the field.

Hilda and Mabel had lived at the Puppy Academy longer than anyone could remember and had taught many young collies the basics of herding sheep. They were gentle, kind, and patient sheep, although they could manage only a slow shuffle around the field these days.

"Now then, young'uns," said

Hilda, "Mabel and I will stand over there." She pointed to the far end of the field. "And you have to run around us and drive us through that gate and into that pen there."

"That pen there," baa-ed Mabel.

"Remember," said Hilda, "run a wide curve and keep it nice and steady."

"Nice and steady," baa-ed Mabel.

Star watched Hilda and Mabel totter across the field. She could feel excitement fizz through her. She was about to herd sheep for the first time—ever. Her paws twitched. Her nose twitched. Her muscles

felt like coiled springs just waiting to bounce.

Star was the last to take her turn. She watched Gwen, then Nevis, then Shep, herd Hilda and Mabel across the field and into the pen. Once or twice, Hilda pretended to hobble away but let the pups herd her back again.

All the time Star was watching them, she felt her muscles tighten even more. She wanted it to be her turn. She wanted to be herding Hilda and Mabel. Her heart thumped inside her chest. The tip of her tail tingled with excitement. She couldn't keep her feet still. She jumped up and down on the spot.

Major Bones waited for Hilda and Mabel to shuffle back to the far end of the field, and then he turned to Star. But before he could say GO, Star was off, streaking across the field in a blur of black-and-white fur. She leaped the fence, did a midair half spin, and flew like a bullet toward Hilda and Mabel.

"Ooh, heavens!" bleated Hilda, breaking into a trot.

"Oh, lordy!" baa-ed Mabel, running off in a different direction.

Star ran around them to herd them up again.

Lordy!

"Ooh, me knees," bleated Hilda, stumbling on a rock.

"Slow down, young'un," baa-ed Mabel. "We're not spring lambs anymore."

But Star couldn't slow down. She was a sheepdog, and she had to herd these sheep. She ran around them in circles to keep them together. Round and round. Faster and faster. Round and round and round and round and round and round and round and round and round and round.

"Ooh! I'm quite dizzy," bleated Hilda.

"My head's spinning," baa-ed Mabel. "I think I need to lie down."

"Me too, dear," agreed Hilda.

"STAR!" bellowed Major Bones. "Come back at once."

Star stopped running. She looked back at Major Bones and then at Hilda and Mabel. What had she done? She hadn't even managed to herd them through the gates. She watched the two old ewes head back to the barn in dizzy circles.

Gwen, Shep, and Nevis were staring at her with their mouths wide open.

Star was supposed to be a sheepdog, the daughter of a champion, but her first attempt at herding had gone horribly, horribly wrong.

2

"Too fast," bleated Hilda.

"Much too faaaast," baa-ed Mabel.
"You almost frightened the wool off
my back."

Star sat down next to the two
sheep, who were lying in deep
straw—recovering.

"I didn't mean to scare you," said
Star.

"We know that, my dear," said
Hilda, "but other sheep won't. If you

go in so fast, they will think you're about to attack them. You're not a wolf, my dear. You are a border collie with sheepherding in your blood. You've got to go in slowly and calmly."

"Calmly," repeated Mabel. "I remember your mom when she was a young pup. Soft and gentle she was. Paws like velvet."

Star stared at her own paws. They twitched

with energy. They wanted to be running, running, running. They wanted to jump and spring and bounce. How could she ever be like her mom? She had so much to live up to.

❀

"Don't worry," said Gwen at playtime. "It will be better next time, I'm sure."

"But we won't be herding sheep," said Nevis.

Star frowned. "Why not?"

"The vet said Hilda and Mabel need a long rest after today."

Shep pricked up his ears. "What will we be herding?"

Nevis looked at them all. "Haven't you heard? We'll be trying for our Level One Bo-Peep badge at the end of the week. But instead of sheep, we'll be herding . . . ducks!"

"Ducks?" said Star.

"Ducks?" said Shep.

"Those quacky things?" said Gwen.

"Yes, ducks," said Major Bones. "Not exactly ideal, but they're the best we can do under the circumstances. I had a word with a few of the village ducks on the pond, and they said they'd do it for a bag of grain."

"But we're sheepdogs," said Star, "not duck-dogs!"

"A true border collie can herd anything," said Major Bones gruffly. "Why, I remember the time your mother herded some human toddlers away from a busy road and back into a park."

Star sighed. She looked enviously at Gwen, Nevis, and Shep. They

were never compared with anyone.
Sometimes she wished her mom
weren't the National Sheepdog
Champion.

Star worried all week. The Level
One Bo-Peep badge was easy.
Everyone said so. In fact, no one had
failed it. But Star chased her tail in
worry. She wished Hilda and Mabel
would be there to help instead of
the ducks. She'd never found the
village ducks particularly friendly.
They spent most of their time in the
water with their bottoms in the air,
ignoring everyone.

It was the end of the week. Friends and family had arrived to watch the pups take their Level One Bo-Peep badge. Star had been practicing all week, running the course with imaginary sheep. She saw her mom and waved a paw. She wondered if the other parents expected Star to be as brilliant as her mom. She wished there weren't so many people watching.

"Quack!" said the ducks crossly. "Quack . . . quack . . . quack . . . quack, quack . . ."

The ducks gathered in an angry group in the middle of the field. Clearly they didn't want to be there. They had only come for the food.

"Quack . . . quack, quack . . ."

WELCOME," yapped Professor Offenbach.

Professor Offenbach was the head of the school. She was a small dog with a loud voice. Too loud, most people said, although no one dared tell Professor Offenbach that.

"WELCOME, FRIENDS AND FAMILY, ON THIS GLORIOUS AFTERNOON. TODAY IS A VERY SPECIAL DAY. OUR FOUR YOUNG PUPS WILL BE SHOWING THEIR DUCK—ER, SHEEPDOG SKILLS. IN THE CROWD, WE HAVE NONE OTHER THAN THE NATIONAL CHAMPION, LILLABELLE OF LANGDALE PIKE."

A ripple of applause spread across the crowd.

Professor Offenbach glanced directly at Star. **"LET'S HOPE SOME OF THAT TALENT HAS RUBBED OFF ON**

A FEW OF OUR YOUNG PUPS TODAY."

Star watched Gwen, Nevis, and Shep take their turns. The ducks were an awkward bunch, running this way and that, quacking rudely at everyone. But each of the pups managed to coax them across the field, through the gates, and into the holding pen, where Major Bones had scattered some grain to encourage them to go in.

Star waited for her turn. Her whole body trembled. Her paws twitched. Her nose twitched. Her eyes focused on the rowdy ducks. They were dabbling in a puddle in the middle of the field, squabbling over the muddiest bit. *Go in slow on velvet feet*, Star told herself. But her body wasn't listening. Her feet wanted to run and run and run.

She was off, racing like a greyhound toward the ducks, her feet flying across the grass, her paws barely touching the ground. She leaped the gate with plenty of room to spare. Too high! Too fast! She went skidding and skittering out of control. Round and round and round she spun.

BAM!

Feathers and mud flew into the air, and Star landed with her face in the puddle.

She picked herself up. It hadn't been the greatest of starts, but she hadn't finished yet. Maybe she could still herd the ducks into the pen. Maybe she could still save face and earn her Level One Bo-Peep badge.

When the mud and feathers settled, Star looked around for the ducks. But they were nowhere to be seen. Nowhere at all. It was as if

they had vanished into thin
air.

Star looked up. High in the
sky, the ducks were getting
smaller and smaller and
smaller as they flapped away
toward the village.

Star felt everyone watching
her. She had nothing to herd
now. She wouldn't get her
Level One Bo-Peep
badge. She would be
the first puppy in the academy to
fail it. She couldn't face any of the
other pups. She couldn't face her
mom, either. Star scrambled up

from the muddy puddle and ran
and ran and ran.

"Funny things, ducks," bleated
Hilda.

"Temperamental," agreed
Mabel.

"They flew away," wailed Star.

"It's their wings that does it,"
bleated Hilda.

"Wings!" baa-ed Mabel.

Star flumped down in the
straw. "What was I meant to
do? Sprout wings too?"

"Star?"

Star looked up. Her mother

had found her hiding in the barn with the sheep.

Star put her head in her paws. "You're mad at me, aren't you? I've failed. I didn't pass the test."

Lillabelle sat down next to her. "Of course I'm not mad. It was only one test. It doesn't matter."

"But I can't herd," cried Star. "I'm too fast."

"Too fast," bleated Hilda.

"Like a rocket," baa-ed Mabel. "An out-of-control rocket," she added as an afterthought.

"It's just excitement," said Lillabelle. "You'll learn."

Star curled herself into a ball. "But you never rushed in when you were young. I'll never be like you."

"Star," said Lillabelle softly, "I don't want you to be like me. I want you to be you."

"You mean fast and bouncy and unable to keep still?" said Star crossly. "Who wants a sheepdog like that?"

"You don't even have to be a sheepdog." Lillabelle sighed. "Just because I am doesn't mean you have to be."

"But what else can I be? I don't want to be a pampered pooch in the city. I want to be outside, running in the hills."

Lillabelle put a paw on Star's shoulder. "Star, you have many, many talents. One day, you will find out what they're for."

But Star wasn't listening. She had

covered her ears with her paws. She
was useless. She couldn't even herd
two old sheep or a few rowdy ducks.
What hope did she have of herding a
huge flock of five hundred or more
sheep? She was no good at anything
at all.

3

"All aboard," woofed Major Bones.

Star climbed into the van with the other collie pups.

Today they were heading off to Hilltop Farm, in the mountains, to earn their Mountain Shepherd badge. They would be herding sheep down from the high hills.

Star sat next to Gwen and looked nervously out the window. "How many sheep do you think we will have to herd today?" she asked.

"They have huge flocks in the mountains," said Gwen.

"Oh," said Star. "I can't even herd a few ducks."

"Don't worry," said Gwen. "You just had a bad day. Anyway, I heard Mabel say we don't have to herd the mountain sheep by ourselves. We'll do it as a team."

"At least they won't have wings," said Shep.

"We'll help each other," said Nevis.

But Star was worried. The others seemed much better than she was at herding. Would it really be that easy, working as a team?

The journey took a long, long time. Star hated having to sit still. Her legs twitched with energy. After midday, the van began to climb up toward the mountains. The road became steeper and steeper and narrower and narrower. Green fields gave way to wide-open mountain slopes of coarse, stubby grass and trickling streams.

"Sheep," said Gwen.

"Sheep," said Nevis.

"Sheep," said Shep.

They couldn't take their eyes off all the sheep. So many sheep. They had never seen so many together at one time.

But Star wasn't looking at the sheep. She was looking up at the mountains, at the way the clouds swirled and danced across the snowcapped peaks. She was looking at the high ridges and the tumbling waterfalls.

She was looking at the way the sunlight played on the dark, wet rock. What would it be like to run up the mountains and feel the sun and the wind in her fur? She wanted to be up there—up in the clouds, higher than the birds. She wanted to stand on the very top of the world.

"Star," said Gwen, giving her a poke. Star pulled herself away from the mountains.

"Look, there's Hilltop Farm," said Gwen.

In the distance, a farmhouse sat at the base of the highest mountain. Major Bones turned off the main road and into the farm's driveway. They bounced and bumped, climbing higher and higher, while the countryside around them became wilder and wilder.

"Oh no," said Nevis, shrinking back from the window.

"What?" said Shep.

"If I'm not mistaken, those are Herdwick sheep."

"So?" said Gwen.

Nevis started to tremble. "My dad told me that Herdwick are the toughest, meanest, scariest sheep of all."

Outside, the Herdwick sheep glared at them as they passed.

All the pups sank lower in their seats. They wished Hilda and Mabel were there instead.

"Welcome to Hilltop Farm." An old, shaggy collie was waiting for them. Thick clumps of hardened mud stuck to the ends of his long fur and clunked together like chimes in the swirling wind. He had a graying muzzle and an eye patch over his right eye. His left eye was as pale as the winter sky.

"Good day, Angus," said Major Bones, shaking his paw.

"Is it?" said Angus, casting his one eye up at the sky. "There's snow in the air. I can feel it."

Gwen looked up at the blue sky. There was hardly a cloud in sight. It didn't look like it was going to snow today.

"I know what you're thinking, wee lassie," said Angus. "But you're in the mountains now." He paused, looking slowly at each of them. "And mountains have their own ideas about the weather."

The puppies huddled closer together.

Angus lowered his voice, as if he didn't want the hills to hear. He pointed to the craggy peak looming above them. "And that there is Stormy Mountain."

"Stormy Mountain?" whispered Star.

"Aye," said Angus. "It lives up to its name. You wouldn't want to be up there when the clouds come down."

Star felt a thin chill of wind curl around her and ruffle her fur. She looked up at the mountain towering above the farmhouse. Wisps of snow whipped up from the mountaintop and swirled in the air. Deep down, Star knew Angus was right. She felt

it in her bones. She wasn't sure how, but she just knew a snowstorm was coming.

"Well, let's get ye all to the barn for a hot drink before we start," said Angus.

Star, Nevis, Shep, and Gwen followed Major Bones and Angus across the farmyard and toward the barn.

"What's with the eye patch?" whispered Shep to Nevis.

Angus stopped. He turned around

slowly to look at them, fixing each with his pale eye.

"When I was a wee pup, laddie, I had a small disagreement with a Herdwick ram," he said. He lowered his voice. "My advice to you is, watch out for the ones with horns."

The pups looked nervously at one another. Nevis's dad was right about Herdwick sheep. It seemed like they really were the toughest, meanest, scariest sheep of all.

4

In the short time it took to reach
the barn, the first few flurries of
snow began to fall.

"Now then," said Angus. He
pointed to a map of the farm. "For
your Mountain Shepherd badge, you
have to gather the sheep and their
lambs up here and herd them down
the hill, across the stream, along the
path, and into the farmyard here.
We'll be working as a team, but I
will be judging you individually."

Gwen, Shep, and Nevis looked at the route Angus had shown them. But Star was looking at the footpaths and sheep tracks that crisscrossed the mountain. Some of the paths led to the very top.

"What about the rams?" said Shep.

"There'll be no rams in the flock today," said Angus. "But you'll have to keep an eye out for ramblers."

"Ramblers?" said Star. She'd never heard of ramblers. "Are they dangerous too?"

"No, wee lassie," said Angus. "Ramblers just get in the way sometimes, that's all. They're people who like to walk up the mountains."

He pointed through the barn doors
to where a group of people in bright
waterproof jackets and pants and
big leather boots tromped across the
yard. They were carrying knapsacks
and maps, and the one in front was
holding a compass.

"What do they do when they get
to the top?" asked Nevis.

"Well," said Angus, "they have a look around for a bit and then come back down again."

Gwen frowned. "What's the point in that?"

"Humans are crazy," said Nevis. "That's what my dad says."

Star watched the people head up into the hills. She didn't think they were crazy. She wanted to climb up the mountain too. She wanted to race across the high ridges and see the whole world laid out before her.

A thin layer of snow coated the ground as they made their way up the steep mountain path. The sheep and lambs were scattered across the hillside. Star tried to count them all. She reached two hundred but then lost count. *Too many to count*, she thought. *How could Angus keep watch over them all?*

In a lower field, a ram with a scarred face and a tattooed ear glared at them as they passed. Nevis stopped to look. He couldn't help staring at the ram's huge, curly horns.

"Oi, fluff ball! What are you looking at?" the ram baa-ed angrily.

Nevis hurried to catch up with the other pups, his tail between his legs. He hoped the ewes wouldn't be quite so scary. At least they didn't have horns.

Star watched the ramblers heading up Stormy Mountain. Some were in small groups. There were others walking alone. She counted ten people in all. People were easier to count than sheep. She secretly wished she could join them.

Angus led the pups across the hills to the lower slopes of the mountain. "We'll need to bring all the sheep down today. There's bad weather on the way, and the lambs might not survive the night if they're caught out here."

Star looked up. Thick white clouds now lay across the sky like a heavy blanket. Flakes of snow swirled down like feathers, covering the ground. Only the long, spiky blades of grass showed through.

Angus sent the pups in different directions to gather the sheep and bring them all together in one big flock. Star was sent to the high slopes, to a stone wall separating the farm from the rest of the mountain.

Star had been waiting for this moment all day. She had been cooped up in the van for too long, and now her legs wanted to run and run. The sheep at the top were happily munching on lichens and moss. They didn't see Star coming. But suddenly they heard her feet racing across the ground, leaping from rock to rock, flying like a rocket toward them.

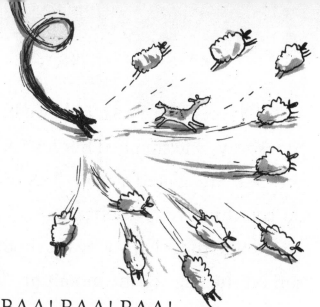

BAA! BAA! BAA!
BAA! BAA! BAA!
The lambs panicked. They scattered
in all directions, their mothers
galloping after them.

Oh no! thought Star. *I'm losing them.*
She ran faster, circling round and
round them, but the lambs panicked
even more, scrambled over the wall,
and charged off up the hillside.

"YOUNG PUP!" An old ewe barred Star's way. She stamped her foot and snorted. She glared at Star. "Just what do you think you're doing, scaring the lambs like that? Do you want them to run off the edge of the mountain?"

Star sat down. She stared at her feet. Why did she have to be so fast? Why couldn't she control herself?

Other sheep started to crowd around Star in a circle. "It's no way for a

border collie to behave," baa-ed one.

"A disgrace," baa-ed another, "leaping around like a wild thing."

One ewe narrowed her eyes at Star. "There's always a bad one—a wolf in every pack."

Star trembled as the angry flock of sheep closed in around her.

"Ahem!" Angus pushed his way through. "Now, ladies," he said. "Break it up. Break it up. There's snow coming. Let's gather up the lambs and head down to the farm."

The old ewe stamped her foot at Angus.

"Please," he added.

"That's better," she said. "Right, girls, gather up your lambs. The old dog's right. Snow's a-coming, and we'd better tuck our young'uns in the barn for the night." She put her head in the air, ignoring Star, and trotted down the hillside with her lamb. The other sheep and lambs followed, glaring at Star with disgust.

Star looked up at Angus. She could see sympathy in his old face.

"Too fast. I know," said Star. She turned and walked away, her head down and her tail between her legs.

The snow was falling faster now, building against the stone walls in thick drifts.

Angus caught up with her. "I hope you don't mind," he said, "but I think it's better if you let the other pups bring the sheep down. It'll be dark soon enough, and we don't want to lose any lambs on the mountain tonight."

Star nodded miserably. There was no way she could earn her Mountain Shepherd badge now.

5

Star stayed at the back of the flock
and watched as the other pups built
up their confidence, running this
way and that, keeping the sheep
together. She followed at a distance
as they came down from the hills,
crossed the stream, and joined
the ramblers returning from the
mountain. The weather was closing
in. No one, it seemed, wanted to be
stuck on the mountain tonight.

The sheep and lambs trotted into the warm light of the barn and began to munch on the sweet hay. Angus stood on a haystack and surveyed them all. "Good job," he said to Gwen, Nevis, and Shep. He looked out at the swirling snow in the darkening sky. "We got them back home in time."

Star knew they'd have to go back home to the academy soon too, dashing her dreams of getting a Mountain Shepherd badge. Maybe she would never be a sheepdog. She was walking toward the barn doors when an old ewe shoved past, bowling her over.

"BAA!" cried the ewe. "Laaaamb!"

"Lamb?" said Star.

The old ewe looked frantically at the other sheep. "I can't find my lamb. Laaamb!" she bleated across the barn. She ran back to the doors. "LAAAAAAMB!" she bleated into the snowstorm. The wind whipped her bleat away, but there was no returning reply.

Angus looked worried. "We must've lost one on the way down," he said.

"Laaamb," wailed the ewe.

Before anyone could stop her, Star was gone, racing out into the gathering darkness, racing out into the storm. Her feet flew across the snow as she retraced their path. She leaped across the stream, circling and sniffing to find the lost lamb. Just beyond the stream, a set of tiny hoofprints left the path. They headed up, up, up, back toward the mountain. The hoofprints went round and round in circles. Star knew this lamb was lost and trying to find its way home.

"Woof," she barked. "Woof!"

A muffled "baa" replied.

Star ran, pounding through the thick snow. If she didn't find the lamb soon, the new snow would cover the prints and they would be lost forever.

At last, she found the lamb lying in a snowdrift, buried in snow, unable to climb out. The lamb was cold and wet through.

"Come on," woofed Star. She put her nose underneath the lamb and pushed it out of the snowdrift.

The lamb struggled to its feet and wobbled after Star. Star waited for it, and together they made their way down the path.

The wind whirled around them. The lamb was weak, but Star gently nudged it down the hill. Sometimes the blizzard blew so fiercely that Star couldn't see her way at all, but she'd kept the map of the mountain in her head, and so she found her way back down.

"Star, is that you?"

"BAAAA!"

Angus, Major Bones, and the old ewe were on their way up the path to meet them. The ewe rushed to her lamb.

"Well done," said Angus. "Your swift feet saved this young lamb."

"Well done, indeed," said Major Bones.

Star sighed. She was glad she'd saved the lamb, but she'd never be a true sheepdog if she couldn't control her feet.

Star followed them down the mountainside and along the main path to the farmyard. The snow had stopped, and a thin sliver of moon peeped through the clouds, lighting the mountaintops. Star stopped to look. She had never seen anything so beautiful. The snow seemed to glow against the dark, star-scattered sky. She wanted to be up there, racing beneath the moonlight across the powdery snow.

"Come on, Star, keep up," woofed Major Bones.

Star turned and trotted down the path. Ramblers' footprints and sheep hoofprints all mixed together in the snow. The rubber soles of the ramblers' boots all left different prints. Star counted nine sets of prints coming down the mountain.

Nine?

She checked again.

She felt a knot of worry tighten in her chest. Her paws twitched.

There were only nine sets coming down, but Star remembered that ten people had gone up the mountain.

She looked back up at the towering peak.

Someone hadn't returned.

Someone was still up there, on the mountain.

It was dark and cold, and another snowstorm was coming.

"Star!" Major Bones called again.

"Someone's stuck on Stormy Mountain," Star called out.

"Star, come back!"

But it was too late. Star was already racing up, up, up the mountain path. Before Major Bones could call her name again, Star had disappeared into the velvet darkness of the night.

6

The path seemed to go on forever.
Star followed the cairns—the piles
of rocks left by walkers to mark the
path. It was much colder up on
the mountain, and the wind blew
through her coat like sharp needles
of ice. Up, up, up she scrambled until
she could go no farther. The whole
of the world was spread out before
her.

The warm orange glow of the barn

light lay far, far below in the moonlit valley.

This was what it was like to stand at the very top of the world. Star wanted to stay longer, but she knew there wasn't time.

Star sniffed around. She picked out lots of human scents and then found one that headed away from the main path, off on its own. She followed it as it went round and round in circles, like the lamb's

hoofprints had. This person was lost too.

Star followed the scent to a ridge that led down the other side of the mountain. But the trail continued to the steep edge of the ridge, as if someone had walked off the mountain and into thin air.

Star crept closer to the edge. She looked over into the darkness. On a thin ledge below her, she could see a lumpy shape. The shape groaned and moved.

It was a young man.

The lost rambler!

He must have fallen over the edge.

"Woof," barked Star.

The rambler turned to look at her. Star could see he was hurt. His leg stuck out at a very odd angle. She scrambled down the rocks, leaping lightly across them.

"Woof," she barked again. "Woof."

The man took hold of her. "Good dog," he said. "Good dog."

Star could feel his hands trembling. They were cold, so cold.

Star knew she wouldn't be able to help the man up. Even if he could walk, he wouldn't be able to climb back onto the ridge above. It was too high and too steep for him.

Star didn't know what to do. She wanted to tell him to wait and she'd find help, but she knew humans didn't understand her woofs and barks.

She couldn't leave the man alone. She sat beside him, trying to keep him warm, but his eyes kept closing. She knew that if he fell asleep, he might roll right off the narrow ledge. She pawed at him and whined, trying to keep him awake. But the night was getting colder. Even with her thick coat, Star could feel the wind's icy fingers. Ice crystals formed on her whiskers, and her breath froze and sparkled in the night air. Somehow she had to get the rambler off the mountain, but how? She knew for sure that he wouldn't survive up here.

She stared out across the valley. What could she do? Her wolf ancestors would have howled across the mountains to find one another. Maybe that was what

she needed to try. Star threw
back her head and howled. She
howled like the ancient wolf that
was somewhere deep inside her.
"AAAAArrrrrOOOOOOOOOO!
AAArrrrrOOOOOOOOOOOO!"

From far, far below came the baying
of dogs in reply.

It was Angus and Major Bones.
They were coming up the mountain
to find her.

AAROOOo

Major Bones and Angus were soon panting on the ridge above Star and the rambler.

Star bounded up the rocks to meet them, her paws light on the crumbly rocks.

"I think his leg is broken," woofed Star.

Major Bones tried to climb down. He put a paw on one of the rocks, but the rock slipped under his weight and went tumbling and bouncing down into the darkness.

"We can't reach him," woofed Major Bones.

"Too far down," said Angus.

"We can't leave him," said Star.

Major Bones pulled himself up to his full height. "Right. Let's go back to the farmhouse and get some help. We can't do this on our own."

Angus nodded. "I'll call Snowdon. He'll know what to do."

"Snowdon?" said Star.

"Yes," said Angus. "Come on! We don't have much time."

Star jumped back down onto the ledge. "I'll stay with the rambler," she said.

Major Bones looked at her. "We can't leave you here too," he said.

"Someone has to stay with him,"

said Star. "Someone needs to keep him warm and awake, and I'm the only one who can get down here."

Major Bones didn't look happy, but he agreed. "Right," he said. "We'll be as fast as we can."

Star huddled next to the rambler to keep him warm.
It was even colder

now, and it had begun to snow again. The clouds covered the moon, plunging Star and the young man into deep, deep darkness. Every time the rambler drifted off to sleep, Star woofed to wake him.

Star wondered when help would come. She knew Major Bones and Angus wouldn't forget her, but it seemed so long since they had left to get help. She was cold, and tired too— so tired. She knew she mustn't sleep, but maybe she could have a little nap. *Just a short one*, she told herself. She was drifting into sleep when she saw a light high up in the sky.

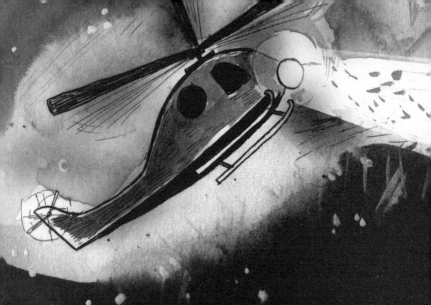

Ducks? she thought drowsily.
Ducks with headlights?

If they were ducks, they were
very noisy ducks, as if hundreds
of wings beat together at
once.

Star opened her eyes wide.
"Helicopter," she woofed. "Helicopter,
helicopter, helicopter."

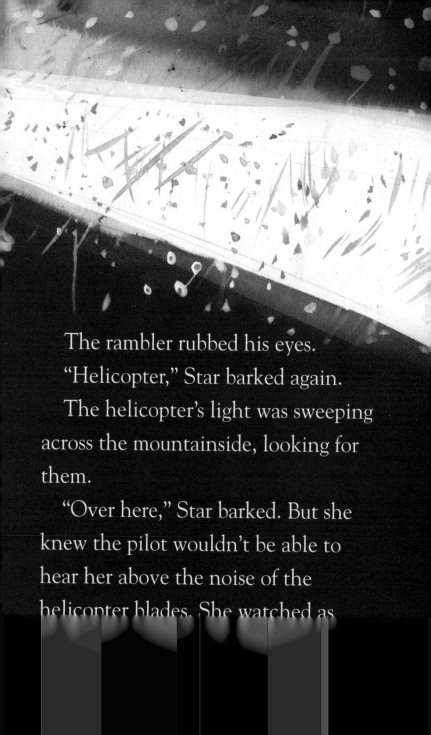

The rambler rubbed his eyes.

"Helicopter," Star barked again.

The helicopter's light was sweeping across the mountainside, looking for them.

"Over here," Star barked. But she knew the pilot wouldn't be able to hear her above the noise of the helicopter blades. She watched as

the helicopter swung away
and started to search another
part of the mountain. The
clouds were coming down again,
and the wind was getting stronger.
The helicopter couldn't fly in thick
clouds. If it didn't find Star and the
rambler soon, it would have to leave
them on Stormy Mountain and
come back the next morning.

But the next morning might be
too late.

The rambler stirred. He fumbled
for something in his pocket. He
pulled out a small flashlight and
switched it on, but his hands were
so cold, he couldn't hold

on to it. The flashlight slipped from his fingers. Star watched it tumble and bounce onto a narrower ledge below, its light hidden by a rock. She knew that if she climbed down, she might not be able to get back up. But this might be their only chance. Skittering down the slope, she reached the flashlight and held it up. She pointed its beam into the darkness, where it shone as bright as any star.

The helicopter turned back, and its light found Star and the rambler clinging to the mountain.

Star pressed herself against the rocks as the wind from the helicopter blades blew against her. She watched a man drop down on a long wire and strap the rambler onto a stretcher.

"Come on, girl," the rescuer said, holding out his arms to Star. "We'll take you back with us too."

Star clung to the man as the winch lifted them higher and higher, right into the helicopter.

"Well done, young'un," said a voice behind her.

Star turned. A big border collie wrapped a blanket around her. She couldn't help staring at him. What was a dog doing in the helicopter? The collie was wearing a bright red reflective jacket. Star had never seen such a thing before.

"Who are you?" asked Star. "What are you doing here?"

"I'm Snowdon," said the collie. "I'm with the Mountain Search and Rescue Team."

7

All the puppies at the academy
gathered for the Friday award
ceremony. Friends and family were
there to watch too. Star sat at the
very back. She could see her mom
looking for her, but she hid down
behind Wolfie, the wolfhound pup.
She didn't want to face her mom
knowing she hadn't earned her
Mountain Shepherd badge.

Professor Offenbach climbed onto
the stage.

"WE HAVE QUITE A FEW AWARDS AND BADGES TO GET THROUGH TODAY," she barked.

"FIRST, I'D LIKE TO CALL UP WOLFIE FOR HIS ACTING PERFORMANCE AS THE WOLF IN THE VILLAGE PLAY OF 'LITTLE RED RIDING HOOD.' EVERYONE SAID HE PLAYED THE ROLE EXTREMELY WELL." Professor Offenbach coughed. "TOO WELL, A FEW VILLAGERS SAID. WE ONLY HOPE THEY WILL FEEL SAFE ENOUGH TO LEAVE THEIR HOMES AFTER DARK AGAIN SOON."

Wolfie stood up to take his place on the giant sausage podium. Star glanced up to see her mom looking directly at her.

"**AND NEXT**," bellowed Professor Offenbach, "**WE HAVE GWEN, NEVIS, AND SHEP, FOR ACHIEVING THEIR MOUNTAIN SHEPHERD BADGE.**"

Star watched her friends gather on the podium. She wished she could be up there with them. She couldn't even look at her mother. Star was the first border collie in a long line of border collies not good enough to be a sheepdog. She had failed.

Star half listened to other pups collecting their awards and badges. Maybe she could slip out of the ceremony. She didn't want to stay any longer.

"AND NOW . . . ," said Professor Offenbach, **"WE HAVE A NEW AWARD. IT HAS NEVER BEEN PRESENTED TO ANY DOG AT THE ACADEMY BEFORE."**

Star crept along the back of the hall to sneak out.

"AND WE HAVE SOME SPECIAL GUESTS TO AWARD IT."

There was a commotion up at the front, and Star could see humans, dogs, and sheep coming through the doors. First was Angus, then the old ewe with her lamb, followed by the rambler in a wheelchair, the helicopter pilot, the rescuer, and Snowdon the mountain rescue dog.

"I WOULD LIKE TO CALL STAR, STAR OF LANGDALE PIKE, UP TO THE PODIUM," barked Professor Offenbach.

Star looked around. Did the professor really mean her?

"STAR, PLEASE COME TO THE PODIUM."

For the first time in her life, Star's feet didn't want to move. They felt like they were stuck in thick, thick molasses.

Gwen was waving her paw at her. "Come on, Star!"

"IN OUR FINE HISTORY AT THE ACADEMY, GUIDE DOGS, SHEEPDOGS, HEARING DOGS, AND MANY MORE HAVE PASSED THROUGH OUR GATES," woofed Professor Offenbach. "BUT TODAY, WE HAVE A NEW JOB TO RECOGNIZE."

All eyes were on Star as she climbed up on the sausage podium.

"STAR HAS SHOWN MANY EXCELLENT QUALITIES. SHE HAS SPEED AND AGILITY. BUT SHE HAS SOMETHING ELSE TOO: BRAVERY AND TRUE LOYALTY IN THE FACE OF DANGER. THE MOUNTAIN RESCUE TEAM SAID

THEY HAD NEVER SEEN SUCH
BRAVERY BEFORE, AND THEY HAVE
AWARDED STAR THEIR HIGHEST
HONOR, THE MUNRO MEDAL."

Angus stepped forward to put the medal around Star's neck.

Everyone cheered. Professor Offenbach had to wave her paws to quiet everyone down.

"AND," she continued, "THEY HAVE ASKED IF STAR WOULD CONSIDER TRAINING TO BE PART OF THEIR TEAM. THEY THINK SHE WILL BE THE PERFECT MOUNTAIN RESCUE DOG."

Star could hardly believe her ears. She could do

something where she could run and run and run across the mountains and feel the wild wind in her fur. Star was standing on the sausage podium, but she felt as if she were standing on the very top of the world.

Professor Offenbach turned to Star. "**WHAT DO YOU THINK, STAR? DO YOU WANT TO BE A MOUNTAIN RESCUE DOG ONE DAY?**"

"WOOF!" agreed Star. "WOOF! WOOF! WOOF!"

"**AND JUST ONE THING MORE,**" said Professor Offenbach, beckoning the old Herdwick ewe onto the stage.

The old ewe climbed up and faced
Star. "The girls and I wanted to say
thank you for saving one of our little
lambs. We got together and made
you a present." She held up a woolen
coat. "Made of the finest Herdwick
wool," she bleated. "It's the warmest
wool in the whole world. It'll
keep you warm and dry out on any
mountain."

"Thank you," said Star, beaming. "Thank you."

Those Herdwick sheep weren't so scary after all.

When the ceremony was over, Star went to find some peace and quiet in the barn.

She lay down in the straw next to Hilda and Mabel.

"Ooh! It suits you," bleated Hilda, admiring the Herdwick coat.

"Suits you," baa-ed Mabel. "Lovely bit of cable knit, that."

"Star?"

Star looked up. Her mom had found her.

"I'm sorry," said Star.

Star's mom sat down next to her. "Sorry for what?"

Star stared at her paws. "I know we come from a long line of sheepdogs, but that's not what I want to be. I want to be a mountain rescue dog. I hope I can make you proud of me."

Lillabelle put her paw on Star. "I have never been more proud of you than I am today. What you did on the mountain was very, very brave. But it doesn't matter to me what you do or how well you do it. I just love you as you."

Star looked up at her mom.

"Really?"

"Really!" Lillabelle smiled and gave her a kiss. "Star, my little pup, you'll always be a champion to me."

Meet Fern, a real-life search and rescue dog!

Name
Fern

Age
9

Occupation
Search and rescue dog

Likes
Tennis ball games, Cheesy Bites snacks

Hates
Cats!

Fern uses her nose to search for missing people. She lets her handler know that she has found someone by barking.

Search and Rescue Dog Facts

Search and rescue dogs use their noses to find human scent, but their amazing sense of hearing and their ability to see in the dark can also help.

It is thought that a single dog can accomplish the work of twenty to thirty human searchers.

Mountain rescue dogs like Star are air-scenting dogs. They pick up a scent on the air and follow it to its source.

 Rescue dogs who travel in helicopters, like Snowdon in the story, must have flight training!

Border collies like Star make great search and rescue dogs, but German shepherds, labradors, and spaniels are also popular.

One of the earliest-known mountain rescue dogs was a Saint Bernard named Barry. He worked in Switzerland in the early 1800s and saved more than forty lives.

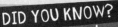

About Ned and his owner, Gill Lewis

I'm NED, a border collie just like Star. My mom was a champion sheepdog too. I was born on a farm in Devon along with seven brothers and sisters. Then I went to live with GILL LEWIS and her family. She doesn't have any sheep, but she does have chickens, and so I love rounding those up instead. I also love playing ball and Frisbee.

My feet never stop. I'm always running, running, running. I always need a job to do. If no one wants to play with me, I play with my best friend, Murphy, a Leonberger. He even puts up with me when I pull his tail. You will see him in a future Puppy Academy book.

But now you'll have to excuse me. I can't hang around here talking—I've got to run!

Henry Holt and Company, *Publishers since 1866*
175 Fifth Avenue, New York, NY 10010
mackids.com

Library of Congress Cataloging-in-Publication Data
Names: Lewis, Gill, author. | Horne, Sarah, 1979– illustrator.
Title: Pip and the paw of friendship / Gill Lewis ; illustrated by Sarah Horne.
Description: First American edition. | New York : Henry Holt and Company,
2017. | Series: Puppy academy | Summary: "A story about a puppy
who is training to be a service dog—and the young human girl he
befriends"—Provided by publisher.
Identifiers: LCCN 2016015268 (print) | LCCN 2016042640 (ebook) |
ISBN 9781627797986 (hardback) | ISBN 9781250092854 (paperback) |
ISBN 9781627797993 (ebook)
Subjects: | CYAC: Dogs—Training—Fiction. | Service dogs—Fiction. |
Animals—Infancy—Fiction. | Human-animal relationships—Fiction. |
BISAC: JUVENILE FICTION / Animals / Dogs. | JUVENILE FICTION /
Action & Adventure / General. | JUVENILE FICTION / Humorous Stories.
Classification: LCC PZ7.L58537 Pi 2017 (print) | LCC PZ7.L58537 (ebook)
| DDC [Fic]—dc23
LC record available at https://lccn.loc.gov/2016015268

Our books may be purchased in bulk for promotional, educational,
or business use. Please contact your local bookseller or the Macmillan
Corporate and Premium Sales Department at (800) 221-7945 ext. 5442
or by email at MacmillanSpecialMarkets@macmillan.com.

Originally published in the UK in 2016 by Oxford University Press
First American edition—2017

Printed in the United States of America by
LSC Communications, Harrisonburg, Virginia

ISBN 978-1-250-21761-5 (paper over board)

1 3 5 7 9 10 8 6 4 2

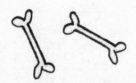

PUPPY ACADEMY

PIP
and the Paw of Friendship

Gill Lewis

illustrations by Sarah Horne

Henry Holt and Company ❖ New York

1

The smell of sausages wafted along the line of puppies sitting in a neat row and drifted into Pip's nostrils. A sausage smothered in thick gravy lay in front of each pup. Saliva dripped from Pip's mouth and formed a large pool at his feet.

Pip willed himself not to look. He tried not to sniff the rising steam swirling deliciously around his nose. He tried to ignore the sausage that was asking to be eaten.

He glanced at the large
bloodhound holding up his
stopwatch.

"One minute to go," barked
Major Bones.

One whole minute! thought Pip.
It felt like a lifetime.

Pip looked along the line of
puppies. No one had given in to the

sausages . . . yet. Maybe they would all earn their Resist Temptation badges. He hoped they would. They had been practicing hard.

They were pupils at the Sausage Dreams Puppy Academy for Working Dogs, where puppies trained for all sorts of important jobs. Some pups wanted to be police dogs. Others wanted to be sheepdogs. There were so many different jobs to choose from.

But Pip knew what he wanted to be. He was a Labrador retriever and wanted to be an assistance dog for a human, just like his mom and dad. His mom was a guide dog for the blind, and his dad was an assistance dog for the deaf. Pip wanted to help people too. He knew that the training was hard and that many dogs didn't make it through.

Every day, he dreamed of receiving the Paw of Friendship, a badge to show that he was an assistance dog and could help a human of his very own.

But first there were many tests to pass and badges to earn, beginning with the Resist Temptation badge. Pip had to pass if he wanted to be an assistance dog. His mom and dad were

watching with the other parents in the academy hall.

Major Bones, one of the teachers, was counting down the time. "Twenty seconds to go . . . nineteen . . . eighteen . . ."

Next to Pip, a little pug puppy licked his lips. His nose twitched. His eyes kept sliding down to look at the sausage.

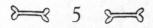

"Hold on, Roly," whispered Pip. "Be strong."

Roly's tongue lolled out and dangled above the sausage.

"Don't do it, Roly. Hold your nerve. Not long now," said Pip.

Roly's eyes fixed on the sausage.

"It's calling my name," he whimpered.

"Resist the sausage, Roly! Don't look at it. You can do it."

Major Bones blew the whistle.

PHHHHREEEEW! "Time's up. Well done, pups. That was a very difficult test, indeed. We'll have a break before we do the final temptation test."

Roly dived on his sausage and slurped it up in a single gulp. "Thank you, Pip," he said, wiping gravy from his chin. "I don't know what I would have done without your help."

"That's okay," said Pip. "I wonder what the next test will be."

Pip was worried. Would it be Ginger the old tomcat, or Peter the mail carrier? Some dogs just couldn't help themselves when it came to chasing mail carriers. But Pip didn't mind cats or mail carriers. He never felt like chasing them at all.

There was one temptation, however, that Pip hoped he wouldn't face in the next test. There was one thing he couldn't resist. He just had to hope it would be something else.

"When you're ready, pups," barked Major Bones.

The pups lined up again as Major Bones brought a small box into the hall. "Inside here, I have something that many of you dream of chasing."

Too small for a mail carrier, thought Pip. Maybe Ginger was inside the box.

Major Bones reached inside.

Pip closed his eyes. He didn't want to see what it was. If he didn't know, he couldn't chase it.

BOING . . . BOING . . . BOING!

Pip's eyes snapped open. It was the unmistakable sound of a . . . TENNIS BALL.

Pip was in the air, leaping for the ball. He snatched it and spun in midair, his legs running as he hit the ground. He raced around the hall with the ball in his teeth, daring anyone to chase him for it.

"PIP!" Major Bones was charging after him.

Pip ran faster, round and round and round. He had the ball, and he wasn't going to let anyone else get it.

"PIP! Stop at once!"

Pip stopped. He dropped the ball and looked around. He suddenly remembered where he was and what he was supposed to be doing. But it was too late. His mom and dad had their heads in their paws. Everyone else was just staring at him. What had he done?

Major Bones shook his head sadly.

"I'm sorry," said Pip. "Let me take the test again. Give me a cat or a squirrel instead."

"You can't take the test again. I'm sorry, Pip," said Major Bones. "You have to resist *all* temptations. What if you had led a blind person into a busy road just because you wanted to play ball on the other side?"

Pip hung his head. Major Bones was right. It didn't matter if he could resist sausages and cats and mail carriers. If he couldn't stop himself from joining in a ball game, he'd be no use to anyone.

He couldn't bring himself to look

at his mom and dad again. He
turned from them and ran.

He'd messed up in one of the very
first tests.

His dreams of being an assistance
dog were over before his real
training had even begun.

2

"I'm sorry," said Suli. "Maybe you could be a sniffer dog, or a search and rescue dog."

"I only want to be an assistance dog," wailed Pip. "What's wrong with me, Suli? Why can't I stop myself from chasing balls?"

"Well, it's good news for us," woofed Star. "We need you in the pawball final next week. Come on, Pip, we've got to run. Gruff Barking and the other teammates are waiting for us on the field."

Pip followed Suli and Star. He didn't feel like joining in, but all that changed the moment he saw the ball in the middle of the pawball field.

It was waiting just for him.

PPPHHHREWWWWW! Gruff Barking, the Puppy Academy sports teacher, blew his whistle for the training to begin.

Pip was off even before the whistle finished sounding. He dribbled the ball between his paws, in and out of the cones. Ahead he could see Star racing into the goal. Star was a border collie pup with lightning feet—and one of the best goalies in the academy. Pip knew he had to get in close before he tried to score.

Left paw . . . right paw . . . left paw . . . right paw . . . Pip took the ball forward, looking for an opening. Nosey, a Jack Russell terrier, dived for the ball, and Lulu, a poodle, tried to tackle, but Pip skipped past them both and knocked the ball into the air. Star jumped for it, but Pip's nose reached the ball first, sending it flying into the goal.

PPPHHHREWWWW! "Well done, pups, well done." Gruff Barking called all the pups together. "Great practice session. You'll need to play like that next week when we're up against the MadDogz in the pawball final."

The five pups of the pawball team looked at one another. The puppies of the MadDogz team were the unbeaten champions. They were young guard dogs from the Security Dog School on the other side of town. They all looked big and scary. It was rumored that Exterminator, their goalie, wasn't even allowed out without a muzzle.

"Do we *have* to play them?" asked Suli. Suli was a saluki pup. What she lacked in strength, she made up for in speed and in her midair turns.

Gruff Barking looked slowly around at them. "MadDogz have been beaten before," he said.

"That was ten years ago," said Lulu. "They've held the Golden Ball in their trophy cabinet ever since."

"They can be beaten again," said Gruff Barking. "You've gotten to the final, so you have a chance of winning. Come on, pups, you can do this. Don't forget who you are!"

"Give me an *S*," woofed Star.

"Give me a *D*," barked Suli.

"Give me a *P*," yapped Lulu.

"Give me an *A*," yipped Nosey.

"Who are we?" The pups high-fived one another and barked, "We're the Sausage Dreams Puppy Academy!"

Pip joined in, but he couldn't help thinking that they didn't sound very tough compared to the MadDogz.

PPPHHHREWWWW! Gruff Barking blew his whistle again. "Right, pups," he said. "Let's try some nose balances."

Pip was just perfecting balancing the ball on the tip of his nose when

Major Bones arrived on the playing field with Pip's mom and dad.

Pip dropped the ball and stared down at his feet. "I'm sorry I didn't pass the test," he said.

"It doesn't matter," said Pip's mom.

"But it does matter," wailed Pip. "I can't take the test again."

Pip's dad sat down next to him. "How much do you want to be an assistance dog?"

"More than anything," said Pip.

Pip's mom and dad looked at each other, and then at Major Bones. "Well, if that's really what you want," said Pip's mom, "Major Bones says he will let you take the test again."

"Really?" asked Pip.

"Really," said Pip's mom.

"That's right," said Major Bones. "But before you take the test, we must be sure you are ready. We have to stop you from chasing balls or playing any ball games."

Pip stared at Major Bones. "Even pawball?"

"Yes." Major Bones nodded. "It's the only way."

"No!" gasped Pip.

"He can't leave us," woofed Star.

"We're playing against the
MadDogz next week," wailed Lulu.
"We need Pip!"

Major Bones shook his head. "If
Pip really wants to be an assistance
dog, he'll have to give up pawball."

"For good?" whispered Pip.

Gruff Barking's whiskers bristled.
"Can't it wait until next week? We
need Pip in the final."

"I'm afraid not," said Major Bones. "I've just heard that a place has opened up at the training center for assistance dogs. Pip has been invited there for a trial period on Monday."

Pip looked around at his teammates. "I'm sorry," he said.

"You don't have to go," said Star.

"But I do," said Pip.

"You don't have to be an assistance dog," said Lulu. "You're so good at pawball; you could turn professional. You could be famous and travel the world."

Pip shook his head. "I love pawball, but I don't want to play it forever. I love people more. One day, I want to make a difference in someone's life. One day, I want to wear the Paw of Friendship on my collar," he said. "I'll do whatever it takes, even if it means putting my pawball days behind me."

"WELCOME TO ANOTHER FRIDAY AWARD CEREMONY," woofed Professor Offenbach. **"PLEASE SIT!"** Professor Offenbach was the head of

the Sausage Dreams
Puppy Academy
for Working
Dogs. She was a small dog
with a big voice. Even Major
Bones sometimes had to tie his ears
beneath his chin when she was
talking. **"IT'S BEEN ANOTHER
SUCCESSFUL WEEK AT THE
ACADEMY, AND I HAVE SEVERAL
AWARDS AND WORK PLACEMENTS
TO GIVE OUT TODAY."**

Pip sat with his friends and
watched other pups climb onto the
giant sausage podium to collect their
awards and badges.

"CONGRATULATIONS TO DUCHESS FOR HER CATTLE HERDING LEVEL-ONE BADGE," woofed Professor Offenbach, hanging a badge around Duchess's neck. "DUCHESS IS VERY LUCKY AS WE'VE JUST HEARD THAT SHE WILL BE VISITING THE ROYAL COWS FOR HER LEVEL-TWO BADGE."

The corgi pup puffed out her chest in pride and readjusted her tiara. She was from a long line of royal corgis.

"AND FINALLY," boomed Professor Offenbach, "I WOULD LIKE TO PRESENT THE FOLLOWING PUPS WITH THE RESIST TEMPTATION BADGE. . . ."

Roly leaned across to Pip. "I'm sorry you didn't pass the test."

"That's okay, Roly," said Pip. "Don't worry about me."

"It's me I'm worried about," whispered Roly. "Gruff Barking's making me play in the pawball final in your place."

"You'll be fine," said Pip.

"Fine?" said Roly. "Have you seen the size of the MadDogz team?

They'll eat us alive . . . literally."

Star gave Pip a nudge. Professor
Offenbach was glaring right at him.

**"IT SEEMS THAT PIP CAN'T
RESIST THE TEMPTATION TO
TALK AS WELL AS PLAY BALL
GAMES."**

Pip tucked his tail between his legs.
He watched his friends climb
onto the podium and receive their
badges. He wished he could
join them up there too.
Maybe he would one day.
He hoped so. But he
knew he wouldn't be
joining them

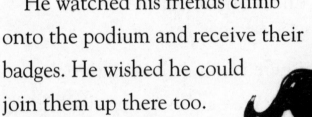

on the sports field next week. He sighed and tried not to think about the final. It felt as if part of him had gone. His pawball days were well and truly over.

3

Pip climbed into the minibus next to Major Bones, ready for the journey to the Helping Paws Training Center in the city.

His friends had come to wave good-bye.

"See you soon," woofed Star.

The minibus rumbled to life and trundled down the hill, away from Sausage Dreams Puppy Academy.

Pip pushed his nose out of the

window. "Good luck in the final!" he barked.

"Bye, Pip!"

"Bye!"

Pip waved and waved as the academy disappeared into the distance. The hills and fields were replaced by shops and houses as they drove into the city. The smells of car fumes and burger joints drifted in through the open window. It was noisy too. There were so many humans in the city. There were no fields to play

in. At least there wouldn't be any ball games to tempt him.

"We're here," announced Major Bones, pulling into the parking lot of the Helping Paws Training Center.

"Welcome," woofed a large yellow Labrador. "Welcome."

"Colonel Custard!" said Major Bones, shaking the yellow Labrador's paw.

Colonel Custard was the head of the training center. He was a retired assistance dog with a graying muzzle, a rickety hip, and a fondness for custard creams. What he didn't know about being an assistance dog wasn't worth knowing.

Major Bones rummaged in the back of the minibus. "Professor Offenbach sent you these," he said, holding out a packet of custard creams. "She knows how much you love them."

"Not for me," said Colonel Custard, patting his tummy. "I must resist. The vets have put me on a custard cream restriction diet. They're not good for the old hip." Colonel Custard looked down at

Pip. "So this is our new recruit, eh?" He gave Pip a good, long look. "So, you're the pawball player?"

"*Ex*-pawball player," said Pip sadly.

Major Bones turned to Pip. "Colonel Custard was once the rising star of the Junior Pawball League," he said.

Pip's eyes opened wide. "Really?"

"It's true," said Colonel Custard, a faraway look in his eye. "I could nose a ball into the goal from ten yards away, doing a half spin." He sighed. "I had to give it all up, though."

"What happened?" asked Pip.

Colonel Custard tapped his leg.

"Bad hips, I'm afraid. That's when I became an assistance dog instead."

"Didn't you miss pawball?" said Pip.

"Not after I met Andy." Colonel Custard smiled as they walked inside. He took out a photo of a man in a wheelchair. "Andy said I saved him, but it was Andy who saved me.

Being an assistance dog to him was the best thing in the world."

Pip's training began with the washing machine. He put his head inside and grabbed a wet towel, pulling it out onto the floor.

"Let's try to get it in the laundry basket this time," said Colonel Custard.

Pip tried again.

All morning, Pip learned new skills. He learned how to open drawers and cupboards. He learned how to take socks off someone's feet and undo zippers on coats. There was so much to know.

"Try the pedestrian crossing button,"

said Colonel Custard.
"You might not be tall
enough yet."

Pip did a
high leap and a
turn and slapped the
button with his paw.

"Well done," cheered Colonel
Custard. "You're a very fast learner.
I think you will make an excellent
assistance dog."

Pip puffed out his chest in pride.

Colonel Custard rubbed his chin.
"In fact," he said, "I know a human
who might be your perfect match."

"Really?" said Pip. He could hardly
believe it.

"Yes," said Colonel Custard. "You would still have to complete your training at the academy, but I may be able to introduce you to your human tomorrow." He held up a photograph. "This is Kayla. She needs an assistance dog."

Pip stared at the photo of a young girl in a wheelchair. "A human of my very own?"

Colonel Custard hurriedly put the photo away. "It all depends, of course," he said,

his voice sounding very serious, "if you can forget all about pawball and ball games. Do you think you can do that?"

"I'll try," said Pip. "I'll try my very best."

"Did you sleep well?" asked Colonel Custard over a bowl of Crunchie Munchies the next morning.

"Yes," lied Pip. He hadn't slept well. He'd had dreams of tennis balls and custard creams and Kayla, all whirling in his head.

"Good," said Colonel Custard, "because today we're going to help you to resist tennis balls, footballs, and soccer balls. You name it, we'll get you to resist it."

"But how?"

"As you know," said Colonel Custard, "I have a fondness for custard creams. I can hardly resist them. So when I want a custard cream, I try to imagine something really big and scary between myself and the custard cream."

"Like what?" said Pip.

"Well . . . like a crocodile."

"A crocodile?"

"It doesn't have to be a crocodile . . . just think of something scary."

Pip thought hard. He thought of Exterminator on the MadDogz team. He thought of Exterminator's huge fangs and wild eyes.

"Here we go," said Colonel Custard. He rolled a ball across the ground. Pip imagined Exterminator standing in front of him. But all Pip wanted to do was get the ball himself. He launched at the ball and dribbled it away.

"No, no, no!" said Colonel Custard.

"You need to think of something *really* terrifying."

Pip closed his eyes and thought hard. He tried to imagine the most frightening thing. And then he realized what it was. The thing that scared him most was the thought of never meeting Kayla.

"I'm ready," said Pip.

Colonel Custard rolled ball after ball across the ground, but Pip didn't

chase one of them. He pictured
Kayla in his mind and knew that if
he chased just one of the balls, he
would never get the chance to be
her assistance dog.

"Well done." Colonel Custard
beamed. "I think you are ready to
meet Kayla."

At the end of the afternoon,
Pip sat in Colonel Custard's office,
munching on a custard cream.

"Kayla will arrive any minute now," said Colonel Custard. "I think you'll be perfect together. I've paired assistance dogs to their humans for many years, and I've never gotten a match wrong yet."

Pip's paws tingled with excitement. He wondered what Kayla would be like.

There was a knock on the office door.

"Come in," woofed Colonel Custard.

The door pushed open very slowly, and in came a young girl using a wheelchair, followed by a tall woman.

"Pip, this is Kayla and her mother," said Colonel Custard.

Pip bounded over to meet Kayla. She was going to be his human! The girl threw her arms up in the air. Surely this meant she wanted to meet him. She wanted him to jump up and lick her face.

Up Pip bounced, again and again, springing higher and higher.

Kayla flapped her hands in the air.

"HELLO, HELLO, HELLO!" Pip barked.

But Kayla couldn't understand his woofs and barks. All she heard was, "WOOF, WOOF, WOOF!"

"Take him away!" she screamed. "Take that dog away!"

Pip ran from the room, his tail between his legs. Kayla didn't like him. Somehow he'd messed things up. But how?

In spite of all Colonel Custard's years of matching dogs and humans, maybe he'd gotten this match horribly, horribly wrong.

4

"Not to worry," said Colonel
Custard, patting Pip on the back.

"She hates me," wailed Pip.

"She doesn't understand you," said
Colonel Custard. "She's never met a
puppy before."

"But I said hello," said Pip.

Colonel Custard sighed. "Humans
don't understand everything we
say with our woofs and barks. She
thought you were attacking her,

bouncing around like that. Humans have to learn what we say with our bodies. If we wag our tails, we're happy. If our tails are tucked between our legs, we're sad or frightened. Sometimes we have to tell them things with our eyes."

"With our eyes?" said Pip. "What do you mean?"

Colonel Custard smiled. "There are no lessons for that, young Pip. You'll just find out how yourself one day."

Pip looked at all the people in the street. Humans were confusing. Maybe the lessons on how to get to

know them would be the hardest
lessons of all.

"Let's try again," said Colonel
Custard. "We'll be meeting Kayla in
her house this time. When you greet
Kayla, sit down, wag your tail, and

wait for her to come to you."

"Okay," said Pip. He followed
Colonel Custard along the streets to
Kayla's house, feeling smart in his
fluorescent yellow training jacket
and training collar.

"Remember, don't jump up or
bounce around," said Colonel
Custard.

Pip nodded, although he thought
it would be hard to stay still for so

long. "Can't Kayla walk at all?" he said.

Colonel Custard shook his head. "Kayla was injured in an accident. That's why she uses a wheelchair now," he said. "She's had many operations on her back, and she hasn't been able to go to school for a long time."

No school? thought Pip. He'd hate it if he couldn't go to the Puppy Academy. He'd feel so lonely. "Doesn't she miss her friends?" said Pip.

Colonel Custard sighed. "It's been very hard for her to go through all those operations, and all that time in the hospital has made it difficult to keep in touch with friends. Her mother said she's lost contact with most of them, and that's been the hardest thing of all."

"We're here," announced Colonel Custard.

Kayla lived with her mother in a small white bungalow. Out front there was a garden filled with pots of brightly colored flowers. A path beside the bungalow led to shops and the park beyond. Pip waited nervously for Kayla's mother to open the door. Would they let him

inside after yesterday?

"Come in," said Kayla's mother with a smile, leading them to the kitchen. She sat down next to Pip and stroked his head. "Look, Kayla," she said. "Pip's a friendly puppy."

Pip wagged his tail even faster.

Kayla glared suspiciously at Pip. "I'm fine," she snapped. "I don't need a stupid dog to help me." She turned her wheelchair around and left the room.

Pip didn't know what to do. He stared after Kayla. How could he be an assistance dog if his human didn't want his help?

Kayla's mother looked at Pip and nodded after Kayla. "Go on, Pip," she said. "Go and find her."

Pip trotted through the doorway, following Kayla to her bedroom at the end of the hall. Kayla slammed the door behind her, shutting Pip out.

Pip knew all about doors now. He stood up on his

hind legs, pulled the handle, and let himself in.

Kayla was sitting at her desk. "Go away, puppy."

Pip sat down beside her.

Kayla glared at him. "Have it your way," she said, "but I don't need your help."

Pip watched Kayla take her pens and pencils out from the drawers on her desk. She had everything at hand. Maybe she didn't need him. She'd managed so far without his help.

Pip lay down next to her and closed his eyes. It was warm with the sun streaming through the window. It was so warm that he began to drift into sleep.

Pip woke up to find pencils and paper raining down on him, and Kayla reaching to grab them back.

The pencils scattered across the floor and under the bed.

Pip picked up a pencil in his mouth and offered it to Kayla, but she crumpled up her picture and threw it in the trash can.

"It was a bad drawing anyway." She frowned.

Pip pushed the pencil onto Kayla's lap.

"I don't want it," said Kayla. She turned away and stared out the window.

Pip collected all the pencils one by one. He had to reach beneath the bed for the last few. He pushed one into Kayla's hand.

Kayla's fingers wrapped around the pencil, and she turned to Pip. "You don't give up, do you?"

Pip wagged his tail.

"So, you think I should draw another picture?"

"Yes," woofed Pip. "Yes."

Kayla sat and looked at Pip for a long time before she began another drawing.

When Kayla struggled to reach a pencil sharpener from a low drawer, Pip opened the drawer for her. When Pip felt Kayla's hands were cold, he fetched her fleecy jacket from her closet.

All the time, Kayla worked on her drawing. When she finished, she held it up for Pip to see.

"What do you think?" she said.

"It's me," woofed Pip.

Kayla leaned forward and reached out her hand.

Pip pushed his head into her hand and let her gently stroke his soft ears. "Good pup," she whispered.

Pip wagged his tail faster and faster. Kayla liked him. She was beginning to trust him, and it was the best feeling in the world.

For the rest of the day, Pip wouldn't leave Kayla's side. He fetched things she couldn't reach. He helped pull her socks off and find her slippers. He even helped her taste some cookies she made. In the afternoon, he and Kayla played in the garden, and in the evening they cuddled up on the sofa and watched a movie together. At bedtime, Pip pulled the covers over Kayla to keep her warm and fetched her book. He jumped up on the bed and leaned against her while she read him a story about a girl named Opal and a dog named Winn-Dixie.

"Good night, Kayla, good night, Pip," said Kayla's mother. She kissed them both and switched off the

light. Pip curled up beside Kayla on the bed. She was his very own human, and he'd do anything for her.

"Pip?" whispered Kayla.

Pip put his head in Kayla's hand.

"I'm sorry I didn't like you at first," she said. "I was just scared, that's all."

Pip whined and licked her hand.

Kayla sighed. "It's as if you understand everything I say."

"I do," said Pip. "You don't know that, but I do."

"You're my best friend, Pip," said Kayla. She hugged him tight and

buried her head in his neck. Pip
could feel her hot tears slide into his
fur. "My only friend."

5

"Excellent!" Colonel Custard smiled. "Excellent. Just as I'd hoped. A perfect match."

Colonel Custard sat with Pip in Kayla's kitchen the next day and ticked off the task boxes on his list. "Open doors . . . tick . . . remove socks from feet . . . tick . . . pick up dropped items . . . tick . . ." He looked up at Pip. "This is very good, indeed," he woofed, ticking off box after box.

Pip wagged his tail. He was pleased he was doing so well. He knew that he would need more training and wouldn't be able to stay with Kayla yet, but they would meet up again several times until he was old enough to be her full-time assistance dog.

"Just one more test," said Colonel Custard, "to make sure you are the right dog for Kayla."

"What test is that?" asked Pip.

Colonel Custard frowned. "It's the most important test of all. It isn't easy, but I think you are ready for it. You must take Kayla up the street, across the main road, past the shops, along the bottom of the park, and back home. You will be crossing busy roads, and you must help Kayla to stay safe. Do well, and you will be Kayla's assistance dog for life. Fail this test, and I'm afraid we'll have to find another assistance dog for Kayla."

"I can do this," Pip woofed.

Colonel Custard smiled. "I'm sure you can."

"I'm not going anywhere," shouted Kayla. "You can't make me."

"It's only around the block. You'll be fine. . . ." began Kayla's mother.

"I'm staying right here," yelled Kayla.

Her mother tried to hand her Pip's leash. "Kayla . . ."

"I'm not going anywhere. Ever." Kayla spun her wheelchair around and stormed to her bedroom, slamming the door behind her.

Kayla's mother sighed and sat down. She put her head in her hands. "I don't know what to do,

Pip. I just don't know what to do."

Pip picked up the leash in his mouth. He had an idea but wasn't sure it would work. He trotted along the hallway and let himself into Kayla's room. He found her sobbing by the window.

Kayla stroked his soft ears and buried her head in his fur. "No one understands, Pip," she cried. "I've hardly been out of the house in the last few years, except to the hospital. I haven't been anywhere on my own before. Not even to the park. What will I say if I meet anyone? What will I do? I'm too scared to face the world right now."

Pip dropped the end of the leash onto Kayla's lap and looked up at her. "Don't be scared, Kayla," he said with his deep brown eyes. "You're not alone because I'm with you now. Trust me. We'll go out and face the world together."

Kayla wrapped her fingers around the leash and looked into Pip's eyes for a long, long time. Then she wiped her eyes and smiled.

"Come on, then, Pip," she said, giving his head a rub. "You and I are going out, together."

"Woof!" said Pip. "Woof!" Maybe

this was what Colonel Custard
meant by talking with your eyes.
Sometimes it seemed as if his human
could understand everything he said.

"Be back before dark," said Colonel
Custard, tapping his watch. "Major
Bones will be here to see you finish
your test."

Pip and Kayla set off together
down the street. Pip could sense her
excitement and worry through her
tight hold on his leash.

It was busy. People moved aside
to let them pass on the sidewalk. All

Pip could see were people's legs and tummies. It was hard to see their faces. He thought Kayla's view from the wheelchair must be the same for her too.

Pip stopped at the crosswalk. The traffic was busy, whizzing past. Kayla let Pip leap up and pat his paw on the button, then they both waited until the green man showed that they could cross.

"Good, Pip," said Kayla.

Pip looked up at Kayla to see she was smiling. They were both enjoying this walk today.

"Let's go to the corner store, Pip,

shall we?" said Kayla. "I'll buy some cookies."

"I like cookies," woofed Pip, although he knew he wasn't allowed too many of them.

Pip walked next to Kayla up the side ramp to the store. The door was stiff to open, so Pip put his paws up and helped to push it wide enough for Kayla's wheelchair to get through. Inside the store, Kayla chose the packet of cookies she wanted. She counted out the money and let Pip put his paws up on the counter to pass her purse to the shopkeeper. The shopkeeper offered Pip a dog treat, but Pip didn't take it. He was a working dog now. He walked with Kayla down the ramp toward the park, his head held high.

They were almost home. Pip could see Kayla's house in the distance. There were no more roads to cross now. All they had to do was walk along the park to reach the path to the bungalow. Pip wagged his tail. He and Kayla were a great team.

The park was busy. There were people walking their dogs and others flying kites. On the far side, Pip could see a group of children playing a game on a rectangle of concrete. A ball bounced on the ground.

BOING . . . BOING . . . BOING!

Pip's paws twitched. His tail tingled with excitement. The children were running around, bouncing the ball and throwing it

between them. It looked a bit like pawball, except the children had to get the ball into netted hoops on the top of very high poles. Two of the children chased the ball as it left the court and rolled across the grass.

Pip stopped to watch, pulling at his leash.

"Basketball," said Kayla. "Looks fun, doesn't it?"

"Looks fun?" said Pip. "It looks BRILLIANT!"

BOING . . . BOING, BOING . . .

Pip bounded forward, pulling the leash from Kayla's hand. "Come on, Kayla," he woofed. "Let's play!" He was off, racing across the park toward the ball. He scooped up the ball on his nose, spinning it in the air, and then he ran to the children, dribbling the

ball between his paws. The children all stopped and pointed, then they charged after him. One boy flung himself on the ground, hitting the ball away from Pip. It flew upward and across the top of the hoop, missing it by inches.

The children threw the ball for Pip again. Pip stopped it with his paw and looked back toward Kayla. She was sitting where he'd left her. "Woof!" he barked. Why didn't she want to join in too? "Woof!"

But Kayla turned her wheelchair around and started heading toward home.

"Woof!" barked Pip. He didn't

want to let go of the ball now that
he had it, so he ran across the park
toward Kayla, dribbling it between
his paws. Behind him, he could hear
the children chasing after him. Pip
stopped in front of Kayla.

"You left me, Pip," she said. "You
left me to be with them."

Pip could see tears in her eyes.
"No," said Pip. He looked at her with
his deep brown eyes. "I came back
because I want you to play too."

"Is this your dog?"

Pip looked up. He and Kayla were
surrounded by a sea of faces.

"He's so cute!"

"Is he yours?"

"He's cool."

"Can I pet him?"

"What's his name?"

"Did you teach him to play basketball?"

"Can he do other tricks?"

"How long have you had him?"

"Do you live around here?"

"I'm Haya."

"I'm Ali."

"I'm Jake."

"I'm Cintra."

"I'm Sophie."

"I'm Luke."

"What's your name?"

"I'm Kayla," said Kayla, stroking Pip's ears. "And this is Pip."

"Cool!" said Haya. "Do you want to play?"

Pip pushed the ball into Kayla's hands. "Woof!" he said, answering for both of them.

Kayla and the children followed Pip across the grass to the basketball court.

"Kayla! Be on our team," yelled Sophie.

The children spread out across the court. Kayla held the ball in her hands. She didn't know what to do.

"Woof!" barked Pip. "Over here."

Kayla flung the ball, and Pip was off, dribbling it forward. Cintra managed to get the ball from Pip and ran with it, bouncing it up the court, but she was intercepted by Luke, who flung it down the far side to Jake.

Kayla spun her wheelchair round and round, following the ball, hitting it in midair when it passed her, or catching it and passing it on.

"Hey, Pip," yelled Kayla. "Catch!"

Pip jumped and spun the ball on his nose before passing it.

"You're good, Kayla!" woofed Pip. "A natural!"

The children played basketball late into the afternoon, only stopping when Kayla shared her cookies with everyone. The sun was setting, and dark shadows slunk across the field.

"Last game," Ali shouted.

He ran with the ball, dodging between the others, bouncing it

close beside him. Pip leaped in and tapped the ball away.

"Hey!" called Jake.

But Pip was already bouncing down toward the other hoop.

Kayla charged after him, dirt flying up behind her wheels, faster and faster. "I'm with you, Pip," she yelled.

Pip was almost there, the other team hot on his heels. Pip and Kayla raced together side by side.

"Woof!" Pip barked, sending the ball up into the air.

Kayla spun around.

Pip saw Kayla reaching for the ball, her wheels spinning beneath her.

Spinning, spinning, spinning.

She was going fast—too fast. Her hand punched the ball, and it flew in an arc in the air. Kayla lost control as her wheelchair flipped and toppled over. Kayla hit the ground as the ball fell right in through the hoop, winning them the game.

"PIP!"

Pip turned. In the gathering gloom, he could see Colonel Custard, Major Bones, and Kayla's mother all running toward them.

Pip looked back at Kayla lying on the ground. He could see grazes on her elbows. He hadn't gotten her home before dark. He hadn't kept her safe. She was hurt, and it was all his fault.

He had failed.

He couldn't resist a ball game.

He would never be an assistance dog now.

Worse still, he would never see Kayla ever again.

6

Back at the academy, Pip's teammates tried to cheer him up.

"At least you're back in time for the final tomorrow," said Star.

"Let's talk about our tactics," said Nosey.

"Come on, Pip," said Lulu. "We'll need to have a plan if we want to beat the MadDogz. They won their semifinal round, fifty goals to zero."

"And the other team's goalie

ended up at the vets'," said Suli.

Pip joined the others, but his heart wasn't in it. All he could think about was Kayla and how he'd let her down. Pawball just didn't seem important anymore.

"WELCOME, WELCOME, EVERYONE!" Professor Offenbach's voice boomed out over the playing field. **"WE ARE VERY LUCKY TODAY TO BE HOSTING THE PAWBALL FINAL HERE AT SAUSAGE DREAMS PUPPY ACADEMY."**

Cheers erupted from the crowd. Dogs from the neighborhood and the academy had turned out to watch the match.

"LET'S GIVE A BIG CHEER FOR OUR OWN SAUSAGE DREAMS PUPPY ACADEMY TEAM!"

All the puppies went wild, howling and barking as Pip and his team ran onto the field.

"AND LET US SAY A VERY BIG WELCOME TO THE REIGNING CHAMPIONS . . . THE MADDOGZ!"

A hush fell across the crowd as the MadDogz ran on. Pip had never seen them up close before.

The puppies of the MadDogz team
were huge, great beasts, with sharp
teeth and wild eyes. They looked
like full-grown dogs. Exterminator,
their goalie, bounded on last. Some
of the pups booed, and Exterminator
bared his teeth at them. *He isn't a dog*,
thought Pip. *He's a monster*. He was
so big that he filled up the whole goal
area. There'd be no way to get a ball
past him.

For the first half of the match, Pip and his teammates spent most of the time running away from the ball. The MadDogz were heavy and slow, but they were scary. Pip didn't dare challenge any of them.

When the halftime whistle blew, the MadDogz were up, twenty to nothing. Pip joined his teammates for a bowl of water. "I wish it could be over," he said.

"I'd rather die than go back out there," wailed Lulu.

"They're not dogs; they're wild animals," said Nosey.

The puppies huddled together

and watched the MadDogz team strutting on the field.

"Who's that?" said Star.

The pups looked across the playing field to see an old yellow Labrador hobbling toward them, followed by a girl using a wheelchair and a group of children.

"It's Colonel Custard and the children from the park," barked Pip, jumping up. "And Kayla. It's Kayla!"

"Hello, young pups," said Colonel Custard.

"I couldn't resist coming to a pawball match. Kayla and her friends wanted to come with me too." He sighed happily. "It reminds me of my Junior Pawball League days."

Pip pushed his face into Kayla's hands, and she stroked him while he sniffed at her wheelchair.

"It's new, I know," Kayla said, smiling. "My last one was damaged in that fall playing basketball. Anyway, I needed this one. See how its wheels are angled so they're much wider apart at the bottom? It won't tip over so easily. I'll need it because I've joined a wheelchair basketball team."

"That's great news," woofed Pip, wagging his tail.

"I know," smiled Kayla. "Haya's mom saw me shoot the ball into the hoop. She said I should take it up. There's a wheelchair basketball club near me. I'm going to play every week."

🐾

PPPHHHREWWWWW!

All the pups looked at one another. It was the start of the second half.

"I'm not going back in," said Suli.

"Me neither," said Nosey.

Pip tucked his tail between his legs and sat down.

"Pups!" said Colonel Custard. "This isn't fighting talk. The MadDogz are a bunch of softies."

"Softies! Have you seen the size of them?" said Star.

"They are big, it's true," said Colonel Custard. "But they are slow and heavy. Use your speed, use your turns, and you can win this game."

"What makes you so sure?" said Pip.

"Because," said Colonel Custard, holding up a photo, "I was on the team that won against the MadDogz ten years ago."

The pups stared at the faded photo of a lean yellow Labrador nosing the winning goal.

"Is that really you?" said Lulu.

Colonel Custard looked around at them all. "They could be beaten then, and you can beat them now."

Pip didn't feel so sure. He slunk around the other side of Kayla's wheelchair and put his head in Kayla's hands. "I'm scared, Kayla."

Kayla stroked his ears and looked deep into his eyes. "Don't be scared, Pip," she whispered. "When I was scared, you gave me courage. You stayed with me. Now I'm here for you. You're not alone, Pip, because I'm with you."

Pip felt his chest swell

up. He might not be Kayla's assistance dog, but he was still her friend, and that meant more than anything.

He would go out there and play his best. He'd do it for Kayla.

"Come on, team," he woofed. "Give me an *S*."

"Give me a *D*," barked Suli.

"Give me a *P*," yapped Lulu.

"Give me an *A*," yipped Nosey.

"Who are we?" barked Star.

The pups high-fived each other. "We're the Sausage Dreams Puppy Academy!"

7

The pups were fast. Star and Lulu whizzed the ball along the ground. Nosey was so small that she could run beneath the MadDogz puppies' legs. Suli's midair turns knocked ball after ball into the goal. The MadDogz were puffing and panting. Some had to stop to catch their breath. The score was twenty to twenty when the whistle blew for extra time.

It was the last chance to win the

match. Pip had the ball. He dribbled it along the sideline. But Exterminator was already in the goal, his hackles raised, saliva dripping from his fangs. How could Pip get past him? Exterminator rushed forward, and Pip nosed the ball high into the air.

Exterminator leaped, his paw outreached.

The ball skimmed the very tip

of one of Exterminator's claws and bounced against a goalpost, spinning into the goal.

The crowd howled and barked and cheered.

When the cheering had died down, Pip looked at Exterminator lying on the ground, clutching his paw and howling in pain.

Pip edged closer to him. "Are you all right?"

"Noooo," howled Exterminator. He held up his paw. "I've split my claw and it huuurts!" he blubbered.

Jaws, the MadDogz team captain, had to sit down and look away. "I don't like the sight of blood," he whined.

Colonel Custard arrived with the first aid kit for Exterminator's paw. "Just like I said," he woofed to Pip. "They're a bunch of big softies, really."

"INSTEAD OF THE FRIDAY AWARD CEREMONY, WE WILL PRESENT THE PAWBALL FINAL TROPHY. PLEASE COME TO THE GIANT SAUSAGE PODIUM, PIP, STAR, SULI, LULU, AND NOSEY," woofed Professor Offenbach.

Pip held up the Golden Ball with

his teammates. He could see Colonel Custard's name engraved in the trophy from ten years before.

All the puppies cheered.

"JUST ONE MORE THING," said Professor Offenbach, quieting them down. **"WE ARE VERY PROUD TO WELCOME COLONEL CUSTARD BACK TO THE ACADEMY. HE WOULD LIKE TO MAKE AN IMPORTANT ANNOUNCEMENT."**

Colonel Custard climbed onto the podium. "We have a very special pup among us," he said. "We have a champion pawball player. Now that Kayla is on the wheelchair basketball team, she will need help to prepare and train for matches. She has asked if Pip can be her assistance dog."

Pip felt his heart leap. He looked across at Kayla.

Star, Suli, Lulu, and Nosey cheered.

Colonel Custard cleared his throat. "But it's not just for his pawball skills that Kayla needs him. It's more than that. It's for the courage he gives her to make friends, have fun, and face the world."

Pip's paws trembled. Could it really be true that he would be an assistance dog for Kayla?

"And so," continued Colonel Custard, "I would like to present Pip with a very special award, given only to those dogs who dedicate their lives to helping humans. I'd like to present Pip with the Paw of Friendship."

Pip stood proudly while Colonel Custard clipped the Paw of Friendship to his collar, then he bounded over to Kayla.

She threw her arms around his neck and buried her head in his fur. "I've got lots of friends now, but you're my best friend of all. I love you, Pip," she said. "I always will."

"Woof," said Pip. He looked up at her and spoke with his big brown eyes. "And I love you too."

Meet Josie, a real-life assistance dog!

Name
Josie

Age
8

Occupation
Child's assistance dog

Likes
Ball games and tummy rubs

Hates
Brushing time!

Josie loves to fetch and pick up things for Sam, who has a severe disability. She's his forever friend. "I'd be lost without her," he says.

Assistance Dog Facts

There are many different types of assistance dogs, including hearing dogs, guide dogs for the blind, and dogs that help people with physical disabilities.

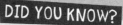 **DID YOU KNOW?**

 It takes almost two years of training for a puppy to learn how to be an assistance dog.

Assistance dogs help give their owners confidence by enabling them to be more independent.

DID YOU KNOW?

 Lots of assistance dogs are Labradors or golden retrievers.

When they retire, assistance dogs normally stay with their owner as a pet.

DID YOU KNOW?

In Italy, there is a 2,000-year-old mural that depicts a dog leading a blind person.

About Sam and his owner, Gill Lewis

I'm SAM, a Labrador retriever, just like Pip. We Labradors love nothing better than hanging out with humans, especially human puppies—they're always fun to be around!

I looked after GILL LEWIS's little ones. I was their faithful companion who traveled with them in cardboard rockets to the moon and sailed with them in a laundry basket across oceans to unknown lands. I listened to them read stories and tell me all their troubles. They were my very best friends, and I like to think I was their best friend too.

Ready for daring
water rescue?

Want to know
about real-life
assistance dogs?

Surf's up!

Henry Holt and Company, *Publishers since 1866*
Henry Holt® is a registered trademark of Macmillan Publishing Group, LLC.
175 Fifth Avenue, New York, NY 10010
mackids.com

Names: Lewis, Gill, author. | Horne, Sarah, 1979– illustrator.
Title: Murphy and the great surf rescue / Gill Lewis.
Description: First American edition. | New York : Henry Holt and Company,
2017. | Series: Puppy Academy | Summary: Murphy wants nothing more
than to be a surf rescue dog like his hero, Boris of Bognor Regis, until he
becomes jealous of a new puppy with the same goal.
Identifiers: LCCN 2016038705 (print) | LCCN 2017018436 (ebook) |
ISBN 9781627798006 (hardcover) | ISBN 9781627798044 (pbk.) |
ISBN 9781627798013 (ebook)
Subjects: | CYAC: Heroes—Fiction. | Leonberger dog—Fiction. |
Dogs—Fiction. | Animals—Infancy—Fiction. | Working dogs—Fiction.
Classification: LCC PZ7.L58537 (ebook) | LCC PZ7.L58537 Mur 2017
(print) | DDC [Fic]—dc23
LC record available at https://lccn.loc.gov/2016038705

Our books may be purchased in bulk for promotional, educational,
or business use. Please contact your local bookseller or the Macmillan
Corporate and Premium Sales Department at (800) 221-7945 ext. 5442
or by email at MacmillanSpecialMarkets@macmillan.com.

Originally published in the UK in 2016 by Oxford University Press
First American edition—2017

Printed in the United States of America by
LSC Communications, Harrisonburg, Virginia

ISBN 978-1-250-21761-5 (paper over board)

1 3 5 7 9 10 8 6 4 2

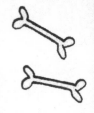

MURPHY
and the Great Surf Rescue

Gill Lewis

illustrations by Sarah Horne

Henry Holt and Company ❖ New York

1

"Help! Help!"

The small Labrador puppy
splashed in the middle of the river.

The pups on the riverbank barked
frantically.

"Pip's in trouble!" woofed Scruff.

Pip splashed one more time before
his head slipped under the water.

There was nothing they could do.

"Oh no!" yipped Star. "He's gone."

A few bubbles rose to the surface

of the water, then all was still.

"Who can save him?" barked
Scruff.

"WOOF!"

A big brown blur whizzed through
the air.

The pups cheered. "Save him,
Murphy," they shouted. "Save him!"

Murphy hit the water.

SPLASH!

He knew what he had to do.
His huge webbed paws pulled him
forward. His thick fur kept him
warm. He swam and swam to the
middle of the river.

He had to save Pip.

He had to.

But time was running out.

Murphy put his head beneath the water, grabbed Pip's collar, and pulled him to the surface.

"Come on, Murphy," barked the pups on the shore. "You can do it!"

Murphy paddled back to them, keeping Pip's head above the water. He was almost there.

Almost!

His paws touched the soft mud.
His claws gripped the ground, and he
pulled Pip out onto the riverbank.

The other pups bounced all around
him. "Hooray for Murphy," they
barked. "You did it! You saved Pip!"

But Murphy was worried. Had he
saved Pip in time?

He looked across at Major Bones,
who was holding up his stopwatch.

Major Bones was a teacher at the Sausage Dreams Puppy Academy for Working Dogs.

"Thank you, Pip, for pretending to be our pup in trouble today. I can now reveal Murphy's result."

All the pups fell silent.

Murphy waited. The river water dripped from his fur and pooled in great puddles around his paws.

"Well, Murphy," barked Major Bones, "congratulations. You've passed your Level One River Rescue. And," he added, "you rescued Pip in two minutes and five seconds. That's a new record for the academy."

The pups cheered.

"You're the champion," woofed Star, "the best!"

Murphy puffed out his chest in pride. He was a Leonberger pup. One day he would grow into a huge, lionlike dog. His ancestors were Newfoundlands, which had once been bred to help fishermen in icy waters. Murphy had water rescue in his blood.

Murphy did what he did best after swimming. He shook himself, starting at his nose, and then his head, and shaking out his chest and body, and then his tail, spraying water over everyone.

"Hey! Watch out!" yelped Star. "You've got most of the river in your fur. We'll *all* look like we've half drowned today."

Pip jumped up and bounced back into the river. "Save me again, Murphy," he barked. "That was fun. Save me again." He swam around in circles.

"No, save me," barked Star. "It's my turn."

"I want to be saved by Murphy," woofed Scruff.

Major Bones stood up. "That's it for today, pups. It's time to get back. If we hurry, we might be able to slip Murphy into the Friday award ceremony."

Murphy and the other pups trotted back to the Sausage Dreams Puppy Academy for Working Dogs. They were in the same class. At the Puppy Academy, pups trained for all sorts of important jobs, such as guide dogs, sheepdogs, and search and rescue dogs. Some pups hadn't even decided what they wanted to be yet.

But Murphy knew.

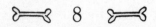

He knew from the very first moment
he had seen Boris of Bognor Regis on
Dog TV, flying across the sand with
the sun on his coat and the wind in his
ears.

Boris was a Newfoundland
surf rescue dog. He
was the only dog
ever to have been
awarded the Gold
Medal of Gallantry
for saving someone
in peril at sea.

Boris was *everyone's* hero.

Murphy wanted to be just like him.

He wanted to be a hero too.

2

"SILENCE, PLEASE!" yapped
Professor Offenbach. "AND SIT!"

Murphy sat next to his friends
in the hall. Some of the younger
pups covered their ears. Professor
Offenbach was the head of the
Puppy Academy. No one knew how
such a loud sound could come from
such a small dog. She could be heard
from two miles away when she was
really mad.

Star nudged Murphy and pointed to a new pup in the hall. "Who's that?"

Murphy stared at the pup. He looked different from the other pups at the academy. He had no fur, except for tufts on his head and tail and at the ends of his four paws. "I don't know," he whispered.

"It looks like we're going to find out," said Scruff. "Look, Professor Offenbach is calling him over."

"BEFORE I GIVE OUT THE AWARDS FOR TODAY'S FRIDAY CEREMONY, I WOULD LIKE TO GIVE A WARM WELCOME TO A NEW MEMBER OF THE ACADEMY. WE ARE VERY LUCKY TO HAVE RODRIGO LOPEZ VISITING US FOR A SHORT WHILE."

Rodrigo gave a small wave to the puppies.

"RODRIGO HAS COME ALL THE WAY FROM MEXICO. I'M SURE YOU WILL ALL MAKE RODRIGO FEEL VERY WELCOME HERE, AND I HOPE

YOU TAKE THE OPPORTUNITY
TO FIND OUT ABOUT HIS
COUNTRY."

"Why's he visiting us?" whispered
Star.

"SOME OF YOU MAY BE
WONDERING WHY RODRIGO
IS HERE," woofed the professor.
"RODRIGO WILL BE
REPRESENTING HIS COUNTRY
AT THE WORLD JUNIOR SURF
DOG CHAMPIONSHIPS AT BLUE
FLAG BEACH. HE WILL ALSO
BE CONTINUING HIS WATER
RESCUE TRAINING WITH
US HERE AT THE ACADEMY.

RODRIGO HOLDS THE INTERNATIONAL RECORD FOR THE LEVEL ONE RIVER RESCUE, IN AN ASTONISHING TIME OF ONE MINUTE AND FORTY-FIVE SECONDS."

Pip turned to Murphy. "Wow," he said. "That's even faster than you."

Murphy scowled. "I could have rescued you faster than that if you hadn't swum so far out into the river."

Scruff tried to get a better view

of the new pup. "And he surfs too! That's pretty cool!"

"Pfff!" said Murphy. "Surfing's no big deal. It's just standing on a plank of wood in the water."

But Murphy's friends weren't listening to him. They were more interested in Rodrigo Lopez, the new pup in the school.

"AND NOW FOR THE FRIDAY AWARDS. LET'S CELEBRATE THIS WEEK'S ACHIEVEMENTS," boomed Professor Offenbach.

Murphy watched Bertie the basset hound receive the Golden Nose award for following a scent trail for

two miles through the woods. He
watched Carly the collie collect the
Bo-Peep badge for herding Hilda
and Mabel, the academy sheep. He
watched Lily the labradoodle collect
the Doorbell prize for alerting a deaf
human to someone at the door.

All the time, Murphy couldn't
help glancing at the new dog. Could
Rodrigo really be that good at water
rescue? Could he be better than
Murphy? Maybe the other pups would
like Rodrigo more. He was probably

one big show-off. Murphy began to wish Rodrigo had never come to the academy.

Professor Offenbach rolled up her piece of paper.

Murphy sighed. Maybe he wouldn't receive his award this week.

"AND LAST BUT NOT LEAST . . ." yapped Professor Offenbach, **"MURPHY, FOR HIS LEVEL ONE RIVER RESCUE BADGE."**

Scruff prodded Murphy with her paw. "Go on," she said. "Go and get your badge."

Murphy joined Bertie, Carly, and Lily on the giant sausage podium.

"WELL DONE," barked Professor Offenbach. She clipped the badge on Murphy's collar. "MAJOR BONES SAYS YOU ARE READY FOR THE NEXT TEST. NEXT WEEK YOU

WILL JOIN RODRIGO AT BLUE
FLAG BEACH BEFORE THE
SURF DOG CHAMPIONSHIPS TO
TRY FOR YOUR SURF RESCUE
BADGE."

Murphy wagged his tail, although
he secretly wished Rodrigo didn't
have to come too.

"AND I'VE JUST HEARD,"
continued Professor Offenbach,
**"THAT YOUR INSTRUCTOR
ON THE BEACH WILL BE NONE
OTHER THAN THE WORLD-
FAMOUS . . ."**

Murphy could feel excitement
fizz right through him. His whiskers

trembled. He didn't dare to hope too much.

Professor Offenbach raised her voice even higher "... **THE ONE AND ONLY ... THE SURF RESCUE HERO ... BORIS OF BOGNOR REGIS!**"

3

The pups packed towels and picnics
into the minibus.

"We're so lucky we can come too,"
said Scruff.

Professor Offenbach had given
all the pups a day at the beach
to watch the World Junior Surf
Dog Championships. Murphy and
Rodrigo would try for their Surf
Rescue badge in the morning before
the surfing competition began.

"Look," said Star, "here comes Rodrigo."

Murphy watched as the new pup struggled with his surfboard and bags to the minibus.

"Come on," said Pip. "Let's give him a paw."

Murphy stayed behind and watched Scruff, Star, and Pip bound over to Rodrigo. They weren't the only ones wanting to help him. Other pups crowded around Rodrigo too. Between them, Scruff and Pip

carried the surfboard, and the other
pups held on to bags and towels.

Murphy picked up his own bag
and climbed onto the minibus.
What was so special about Rodrigo?
He flumped down on a seat and
hoped his friends would join him.
Many pups took seats around
Rodrigo, but Star, Scruff, and Pip sat
down next to Murphy.

"Have you seen Rodrigo's
surfboard?" said Star.

"It was designed by Salty Old Sea

Dogs, the best surfboard makers in the world," said Scruff.

"Rodrigo says it's a triple-finned shortboard, for faster turns on the waves," said Pip.

Murphy pretended to yawn. "Wow, that's sounds *really* interesting." He turned around to look at Rodrigo. Rodrigo's sun-bleached fur flopped over his eyes.

"He looks pretty cool, doesn't he?" sighed Scruff.

Murphy snorted. "More like a rat with a bad-hair day."

"Murphy!" said Star. "That's a mean thing to say."

"Well, look at him," said Murphy. "He's got hardly any fur on him."

"He's not supposed to," said Pip. "He's a Mexican Hairless dog."

"Brainless too, probably," muttered Murphy.

"Don't be like that," said Star. "He seems nice and really friendly."

"He's a great surf dog too," said Pip.

Murphy scowled and turned away. "If he's so wonderful, why don't you go and sit with him instead?"

Star grabbed her bag and got up. She looked at Murphy with hurt in her eyes. "Well, maybe we will." She turned to the others. "Come on, let's go and see Rodrigo. I'm not sure we're welcome here."

Star, Scruff, and Pip moved seats, leaving Murphy on his own, all alone.

Murphy could see Major Bones glancing back at him, but Murphy pretended he couldn't care less. He stared out the window at the passing hills and fields as the minibus bumped along, and he tried to ignore all the jumbled-up feelings bouncing around, deep down inside him.

As the minibus came down the hill to Blue Flag Beach, Murphy stared

out across the sea. It was the very
first time he had ever seen the sea,
which was bigger and bluer and
sparklier than he had ever imagined.

It was a perfect beach day: warm
and breezy. The water glittered in
the early morning sunshine. The
parking lot was filling up. People
and dogs were spilling out of cars

with surfboards, bags and towels, and buckets and shovels. It was going to be busy on the beach today.

"NOW THEN, PUPS," boomed Professor Offenbach, "THIS IS A LIFEGUARDED BEACH, BUT TAKE NOTE OF THE DIFFERENT FLAGS. SWIM ONLY BETWEEN THE RED-AND-YELLOW-STRIPED FLAGS, AND NO SWIMMING WHEN THE RED FLAG IS FLYING."

"Come on," yelled Star, climbing out of the minibus. "Let's find a spot on the beach where we can watch the surf dog championships later."

Murphy stayed behind with

Rodrigo and Major Bones while the other pups ran off across the beach with Professor Offenbach. Toward the far end of the beach, bright banners with WORLD JUNIOR SURF DOG CHAMPIONSHIPS rippled in the breeze. Already there were lots of pups with surfboards of all shapes and sizes lined up on the sand.

The ocean was calm. Small waves curled and ran along the shoreline.

"These waves are too tiny!" cried Rodrigo. "I cannot surf on them!"

"Maybe the competition will be canceled," said Murphy. He secretly hoped it would be, so that Rodrigo wouldn't get the chance to show off in front of the other pups.

"¡*Qué problema!*" said Rodrigo. "I have come so far for this."

"Don't worry," woofed Major

Bones. "The surf forecast says the wind will pick up. There will be some big waves this afternoon."

"That is good news," said Rodrigo. "I've been looking forward to seeing Aliikai catch some waves."

"Aliikai?" said Murphy. "Who's Aliikai?"

"Aliikai?" said Rodrigo, flicking his mop of fur from his eyes. "You haven't heard of her? She is the world junior surf dog champion from Hawaii. She lives up to her name. It means 'Queen of the Sea.'"

"Is she better than you?" said Murphy.

Rodrigo's eyes lit up. "*Amigo*, she's the best. It would be an honor to surf on the same wave as her."

"Right, you two," barked Major Bones at Murphy and Rodrigo. "Come with me. It's the moment you've been waiting for. We're off to meet the world-famous surf rescue dog, Boris of Bognor Regis."

Murphy trotted across the sand, wagging his tail in excitement. He followed Major Bones up the wooden steps leading to the lifeguard hut.

The human lifeguards patted the pups' heads as they passed.

"Pups!" announced Major Bones. "May I introduce you to Boris of Bognor Regis."

"Welcome to Blue Flag Beach," said Boris.

Murphy just stared at his hero. He couldn't think of anything to say. The sea breeze lifted Boris's silky black fur, and the sunlight glinted

in his deep brown eyes. The Gold
Medal of Gallantry around his neck
shone brightly. He looked even more
magnificent than he did on TV.

Murphy closed his eyes and
imagined Boris placing a gold medal
around his own neck.

"*¡Qué vista!*" said Rodrigo.

"Yes," agreed Boris. "It's a fine
view. From here we can see along
the whole beach. It's important to
keep watch at all times."

Murphy shook himself from his
daydream and looked down the
length of Blue Flag Beach. It
stretched in a long curve of yellow

sand between two headlands. The tide was out. The sea was a vivid blue. It glittered and sparkled beneath the hot sun. Small waves broke on the shore, foaming across the wet sand. The beach was busy now. It was a patchwork of brightly colored towels and striped umbrellas. Murphy could see his puppy friends playing on the sand. Humans were everywhere too: sitting in beach chairs, playing ball games, flying kites. There were lots of people in the water, running in and out, jumping over the small waves, swimming, and lying on bodyboards. *So many people*, thought Murphy. *How could Boris and the human lifeguards possibly watch over them all?*

"So," said Boris. "Before we head into the water, let's have a little theory test."

Murphy glanced at Rodrigo. He wanted to show Boris that he knew his stuff. He wanted to answer the questions before Rodrigo.

Boris pointed to the ocean with his huge paw. "Tell me, young pups, what dangers are out there in the sea?"

Murphy shot his paw in the air. "There might be jellyfish on the sand or in the water?" he said.

"Very good," said Boris. "The tentacles of a jellyfish can cause a very painful sting. What else? What about the sea? Is it safe out there today?" Murphy and Rodrigo looked up and down the beach. Murphy knew it was dangerous to swim around headlands because of strong currents, but it was low tide. The sea was calm, and the waves were small. Rodrigo put his paw in the air, but Murphy answered before

Rodrigo had a chance. "It's quite safe out there," said Murphy. "It's perfect for swimming."

"Young pup," said Boris, clearing his throat. "NEVER for one moment think the sea is safe. It may be a fun place to play, but there are ALWAYS dangers."

"But . . . it looks so calm," said Murphy.

Boris shook his head. "Out there lies DANGER. INVISIBLE. UNSEEN. Something with the power to take you out to sea."

"Sharks?" said Murphy.

"I'm not talking about sharks," said Boris. "Let's see if Rodrigo has the right answer."

Rodrigo put his paws on the wooden railings, then pointed to the very far end of the beach. "Over there," he said, "where the waves look a bit flattened. That might be a rip current."

"Well done." Boris beamed. He held up a board with a diagram of a rip current. "Can you tell us what a rip current is, and what you do if you get stuck in one?"

Rodrigo cleared his throat. "It's a fast-moving current of water that moves away from the beach. If you get caught in one, don't try to swim against it. You must swim along, parallel to the beach, until you are out of it, and then swim to shore."

"Well done, well done," said Boris, patting Rodrigo on the back.

Murphy turned away and scowled. He wanted to prove he was better than Rodrigo. He had to find a way he could impress Boris too.

4

"So," said Boris, "what should humans do if they find themselves in trouble in the water?"

Murphy put his paw up. "They should wave a hand in the air and shout for help."

"Well done," said Boris. "Let's just spend a while looking out across the bay, checking that no one is in trouble."

Murphy puffed out his chest in

pride. He'd gotten an answer right.
He stood at the top of the steps and
surveyed the beach, just like his
hero. He felt the sun on his back
and breathed in the salt smell of
the sea. This had to be the best job
in the whole wide world. This was
where he belonged. This was where
he'd always wanted to be.

He watched humans enjoying
their picnics. He looked beyond the
puppies from the academy, who were
lying on the sand, to a boy building
a sandcastle on the beach. No one
needed help today. Or did they?

Beyond the sandcastle, Murphy

could see two small children yelling
and splashing in a big rock pool. The
water came right up to their necks.
One girl went under the water and

disappeared from sight. She waved
her hands wildly in the air. The
humans around her didn't notice.

The children needed help, and they needed it now. Murphy glanced at Rodrigo and Boris, but they were looking the other way. Maybe this was his chance to prove himself. This was a real-life rescue.

Murphy leaped down the wooden steps and bounded across the beach. He felt the wind in his ears and the sand beneath his feet. This was it— this was his moment. This was when he would make Boris proud. His friends would see he was much better than Rodrigo. People would gather around him and cheer. He'd be Murphy, surf rescue pup: the hero of the day.

"Woof," Murphy barked. "I'm coming. . . . Woof! Woof! Woof!"

The puppies from the academy scattered as sand flew up from Murphy's paws.

He slammed through the sandcastle.

He pounded through the picnics.

Nothing else mattered now, only the rescue.

Murphy took a flying leap and splashed into the middle of the rock pool. It wasn't deep at all. The water only came up to his knees. The girls screamed and scrambled out of the rock pool.

Murphy ran after them. "Wait, wait!" he barked.

But the girls ran faster and faster. Murphy felt Boris grab his collar and pull him back. "Not so fast, young pup. Don't scare them. They didn't need saving."

Murphy stared after them. "But the water looked so deep. It came up to their necks."

"They were lying down," said Boris, sighing.

Rodrigo and the other pups crowded around him. Murphy thought he heard a few of them snickering.

"But the children were shouting and splashing and waving their arms in the air," said Murphy. "They needed help."

Boris put a big paw on Murphy's shoulder. "Children scream and shout on the beach. It's what they do. They are just having fun. You must learn to tell the difference between who is in trouble and who is just having a good time."

"I told them to wait, but they ran away even faster," said Murphy.

Boris sighed. "Humans can't understand our woofs and barks," he said. "You know that. The children were frightened of you charging at them like that."

Murphy stared down at his own large paws. He'd messed up again.

He'd made a fool of himself in front of Boris and in front of his friends. There was so much to learn. Maybe he just wasn't good enough to become a surf rescue dog. Maybe he wasn't good at anything at all.

"Cheer up, Murphy," said Boris. "It was an easy mistake. Let's get in the water and start your rescue training. Would you like that?"

Murphy nodded. At least swimming was one thing he knew he could do.

"Good," said Boris, "but first,

I will need you to put on one of these." He held up a water rescue jacket. "This will help you float in rough seas, and these handles are for the human to hold on to. Hopefully both you and Rodrigo will earn your Surf Rescue badges today."

Boris checked that the human lifeguards were watching the beach, and then he led Murphy and Rodrigo down to the water's edge.

"Right," said Boris. "I will swim out beyond the breaking waves and then wave my paws as the signal to rescue me. To earn your Surf Rescue badge, you must swim out to me and pull me back to shore. Is that clear?"

Murphy nodded. He'd trained for this. He'd read all the books. He was the best swimmer at the academy. He'd rescued pups from the swimming pool and from the river. He felt ready.

Almost.

The only thing he had never done was swim in the sea!

Since they arrived at the beach, the wind had picked up and the waves were bigger. White foam crested their tops.

The waves looked much bigger from the shoreline. They looked HUGE.

He didn't feel so sure about swimming in the sea now.

"Who wants to go first?" asked Boris.

Murphy waited for Rodrigo to put his paw in the air.

"Good luck, Rodrigo," said Boris.

As Boris trotted into the sea, a boy in a red baseball cap and Hawaiian shorts ran after him and tried to ride on his back.

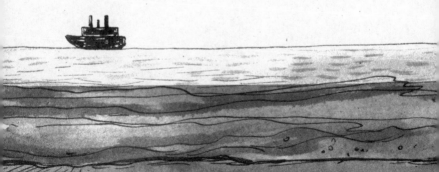

"Save me! Save me!" the boy shouted.

Boris had to bark at him to make him let go. He left the boy in the shallows and swam out beyond the breaking waves. He faced the shore and put his paws in the air. This was the signal. He needed rescuing.

Rodrigo plunged into the water. He was only a little dog, but he paddled out through the surf. Wave after wave passed over Rodrigo. The little dog disappeared and bobbed up again, swimming out to Boris.

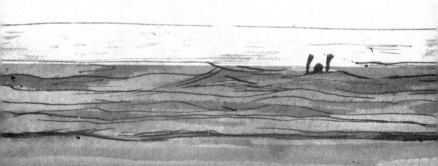

Murphy watched as Boris grabbed onto the handle of the water rescue jacket with his teeth and let Rodrigo pull him back to shore.

"Perfect!" woofed Boris when they were back on the beach. "Textbook stuff. Well done."

Rodrigo took off his jacket and shook himself dry. "Good luck," he barked at Murphy.

Murphy looked out at the waves. If Rodrigo could do it, surely he could too. Rodrigo looked more like a lap dog than a water rescue dog.

The boy in the red baseball cap hadn't given up. He lay down in the shallow waves and kicked and thrashed in the water, pretending to be in trouble. "Save me! Save me!" he yelled. Boris ignored him and swam back into the sea.

Murphy waited until Boris gave the signal, and then he plunged in. He bounded over the waves in the shallows. But the water was getting deeper and the waves were getting higher. Soon Murphy was out of his depth. He kept losing sight of Boris behind each wave. Spray splashed in his eyes, and the sea caught his legs and swirled him round. How had Rodrigo managed to keep swimming in this?

One wave rose up in front of him—up and up and up. Murphy tried to swim over the top of it, but it began to curl, then folded on top of him, rolling him over and over and over. He closed his eyes. Water rushed into his mouth and up his nose. It was like being in a giant washing machine at full spin.

Round and round and round and round and round he spun, until the wave tumbled him all the way back to the beach and dumped him on the hard sand.

Murphy opened his eyes to see Major Bones, Rodrigo, and all his friends staring down at him.

"What happened?" said Star.

"Are you okay?" said Rodrigo.

Murphy groaned and closed his eyes. He'd made a fool of himself again. He couldn't get anything right.

Major Bones leaned down. "Up you go, Murphy. Let's get you back into the sea."

Murphy looked at the waves. They looked even bigger than before. He didn't want to face the waves ever again. Not even the little ones. He didn't want to mess up again in front of his friends. He wasn't sure he even wanted to be a surf rescue dog anymore. He had to face it: he was scared of the sea. "I think I'll be a lifeguard at a swimming pool instead," he said.

"Don't be silly," said Star.

"Have another go," said Scruff.

"No!" wailed Murphy.

Boris pushed his way through the pups. "Do you want to try that again?"

Murphy covered his face with his

paws. He'd failed in front of his hero.
What if he failed a second time? "I'm
not going back out there."

"Amigo," said Rodrigo, patting
Murphy's back, "do it for your
friends."

Murphy looked at them all and
then glared at Rodrigo. "They don't
need me now, anyway, because they
have you."

"Murphy—!" said Star.

"Just leave me," Murphy blurted
out. He flung off his water rescue
jacket, pushed his way through the
pups, and ran and ran to the far end
of the beach. He sank down behind

the rocks, closed his eyes, and pressed his head against the sand, hoping it would swallow him up. His friends wouldn't think he was a hero anymore. It was all over. His dreams were crushed. He'd never be a surf rescue dog—not now, not ever.

Everything had gone horribly, horribly wrong.

5

Murphy lay still for a long time. He hoped everyone would forget about him and leave him there forever.

Just as he was beginning to wonder if everyone *had* forgotten about him, a shadow passed across his face.

"Hey, amigo!"

Murphy opened one eye.

Rodrigo was standing over him, leaning against his surfboard.

"What do you want, Rodrigo?"

"I came to see if you'd like to catch some heavies with me before the competition starts?"

"Heavies?" said Murphy.

"¡Sí! Let's go find ourselves some big waves."

"I told you. I'm not going back in," said Murphy. He stared at the waves thundering on the shore. "I can't believe you actually like it out there."

"I didn't always like it," said Rodrigo.

"You didn't?" said Murphy.

"No," said Rodrigo. He sat down on the sand next to Murphy. "Where I come from, everyone surfs. When I first tried, the other dogs were always better than me. I wanted to be the best so much that I didn't enjoy just being out on the water. I kept falling off the big waves. I was frightened!"

"Then what happened?" said Murphy.

"Well, I stayed on the shore

while I watched my friends surfing. Some were better than others, but it didn't seem to bother them. They were all having fun. I realized I wasn't frightened of the waves. I was frightened of failing. I was frightened of not being the best."

"So what did you do?"

"I figured that I didn't have to be *the* best, but I had to try to be *my* best," said Rodrigo. "Take Aliikai. I may never be as good a surfer as she is, but I can learn from her. Now I just try to get a little bit better every day, and best of all, I have fun with my friends too."

Murphy stared at his paws for a long, long time. "I'm sorry I haven't been very nice to you. I wanted to be the best. And I wanted my friends to like me. I was worried they'd like you more."

"Your friends *do* like you."

Murphy turned around to Star's voice.

"Star!" said Murphy.

The other pups were there too.

"Of course we like you, Murphy," said Pip.

"We don't like you just because you're great at water rescue," said Star. "You don't have to be a hero for us to want to be your friends. We like you because you're you."

"But you haven't been very nice since Rodrigo arrived," said Scruff.

"I know," said Murphy, "and I'm sorry. Can you forgive me?" Murphy looked at all his friends.

"Of course," they barked.

"Thank you," woofed Murphy. "Thank you."

"Hey, amigo!" said Rodrigo, slapping

Murphy on the back. "Surf's up.
C'mon. Hitch a ride with me."

Murphy's paws trembled. The waves
looked like big monsters rising up to
eat him. "I can't go back out there."

"Go on," said Star. "You do want
to be a surf rescue dog, don't you?"

Murphy swallowed hard and
nodded. He wanted to be one more
than anything in the world.

Rodrigo leaned in close. "There is an old sea dog saying: 'If you want to see what's on the other side of the ocean, you have to leave the shore.'" Rodrigo held out a paw. "It means that sometimes you have to be brave enough to take the first step."

Murphy shook Rodrigo's paw, then followed him back along the beach and into the shallow waves.

"Hop up behind me," said Rodrigo.

Murphy climbed behind Rodrigo on the surfboard. It wobbled, but he clung on, lying low, and they paddled out to sea.

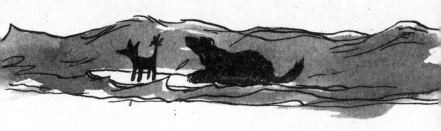

Rodrigo pointed to the breaking waves. "Keep your head down when the breakers come at you and let them pass over," he said. "And if you meet a really big one, turn turtle!"

"Turn turtle?" said Murphy.

A huge wave curled over and its foam surged toward them.

"*Sí*," said Rodrigo, "like this. Hold on tight, amigo!" He flipped the board so they were underneath the surfboard as the wave passed over them. Then he flipped them back up again. "That way you don't end up in a wipeout."

Murphy watched the wave tumble on its way toward the shore.

Rodrigo paddled them out beyond the breaking waves, and Murphy sat with him on the board, rising up and gliding down in the swells.

Wave after wave rolled in from the ocean.

"You ready to catch one?" asked Rodrigo.

"I've never tried surfing before," said Murphy. "Is it scary?"

"There's nothing like it," said Rodrigo. "You've got to listen to the ocean. Hear its voice inside of you. Become part of the wave, part of the ocean."

Rodrigo paddled them toward the shore. He turned around to look at the oncoming waves. A big one started to rise up and up behind them. "This is our wave, amigo. Stay with me."

Murphy paddled with Rodrigo. As the wave caught them, the surfboard teetered on the crest, and then they were over the top of it, rushing down the other side, faster and faster. Murphy's ears streamed out behind him. The salty wind

ran through his fur. He felt like he
was flying! It was the best feeling in
the world. Nothing else mattered. He
knew what Rodrigo meant. He was
part of the wave, part of the ocean.

"ARRRRRROOO!" howled Rodrigo.

"ARRRRRROOOO!" howled
Murphy.

They whizzed in a blur of dog and
surf toward the shore.

Murphy jumped off in the
shallows and bounced around the
surfboard. "That was amazing!" he
barked. "Let's do it again."

By the time Murphy and Rodrigo heard Boris calling their names, they had already ridden about twenty waves.

"It seems you have mastered the waves," said Boris. "Maybe you should try for your Surf Rescue badge after all. We just have time for the test before the surf dog competition starts."

Murphy couldn't believe his ears. Maybe he could still be a surf rescue dog! "Thank you, Rodrigo," he said. "Thanks for everything."

Major Bones and Rodrigo helped

Murphy into his water rescue jacket again, while Boris swam out to be rescued. The boy in the red baseball cap was back and tried even harder to grab hold of Boris, but Boris just shook him off and pushed him back to the beach.

Murphy watched the boy wander down the shoreline with his hands deep in the pockets of his shorts, kicking the waves with his feet. He kept turning around, glaring moodily back at them.

Boris paddled out beyond the breaking waves. "Right," he barked. He bobbed up and down and waved his paws in the air. "Come on, Murphy. Let's see what you can do."

"HELP! HELP!"

Murphy turned to look farther down the beach. The boy with the red baseball cap was in the water,

and he seemed quite far out. The water was up to his neck, and the waves were crashing over him. He disappeared for a moment, then came back up flailing his hands in the air.

"HELP! HELP!"

Boris was already swimming toward the boy. "Stay on the beach, pups!" he barked. "This is an emergency. This is the real thing."

6

Murphy watched Boris paddle toward the boy. His thick black fur streamed out behind him. The boy went under again. Murphy held his breath. He was watching his hero in action. This was a real rescue. He hoped he would be as brave one day too.

People lined the shore and watched as Boris fought his way through the waves. He had almost reached the boy when the boy suddenly stood up. Boris soon found himself walking in shallow water too. They were on a sandbar, and the water was only ankle deep. The boy had been pretending to be in trouble.

The boy started laughing and pointing at Boris, but Boris just turned and headed back to the shore. His fur dripped with water and seaweed, but he looked too angry to even shake himself off.

Back at the lifeguard hut, Boris shook himself dry. "It's very dangerous

to distract the emergency services like that. His silly game could have cost the lives of others."

Murphy glanced back out to sea. The surf dog competitors were lined up on the sand, and a large golden retriever with sun-bleached fur looked ready to announce the start of the competition. "What about my Surf Rescue badge?" asked Murphy.

Boris shook his head. "I'm afraid we won't have time now, Murphy. The competition is about to begin, and it will be too late afterward to try."

Murphy sighed. He had wanted to earn his Surf Rescue badge today. He followed Boris down to the shore and helped him move the black-and-white checkered flags along the beach to show where the surfing competition would take place.

Murphy passed Rodrigo. "I hope you win."

"Thanks," said Rodrigo. "I hope so too, but look over there. That's Aliikai, the world champion."

A small Chihuahua was polishing a pink surfboard.

Murphy patted Rodrigo on the back. "Good luck, amigo! Do your best."

Murphy didn't sit with his friends. He stayed on duty with Boris to watch over the competition and make sure none of the competitors got into difficulties.

Murphy watched Rodrigo take his turn. All the pups at the academy cheered for him. Rodrigo paddled out and caught a wave, slicing down its breaking edge. He put in a couple of good turns. It was good, but was it good enough to win?

Dog after dog went up to surf.

Alfonso the affenpinscher from California wiped out under a big wave.

Lara the lurcher from Cornwall tipped the front of her board into a wave and went flying through the air.

All the time the waves were getting bigger and bigger.

"Look," said Boris. "It's Aliikai's turn now."

Everyone on the beach clapped and cheered as Aliikai made her way down to the water's edge. Excitement rippled across the crowd. They were about to see the world champion in action. No one

wanted to miss this. All eyes were
on the small Chihuahua and the
pink surfboard as Aliikai paddled
out into the waves.

Murphy surveyed the beach.
No one else was in the water.
Everyone had gathered to watch the
competition. The sea was empty.
Empty—except for one boy . . . the
boy in the red baseball cap.

The boy was in the water at the far end of the beach, waving his arms in the air.

"Look," said Murphy. "That boy's calling for help again."

Boris stared across the beach.

"Hmmph!" he said. "The nerve of him. He's fooling around again, wanting attention. Best ignore him. He'll come out when he's bored."

Boris trotted away to make sure he was in a position to help Aliikai if she needed it.

But Murphy couldn't ignore the boy. He was waving his hands wildly

above his head. Murphy was sure he was calling out too, although the wind was blowing away from him, carrying the boy's voice farther down the beach in the other direction.

A colder wind was blowing, ruffling Murphy's fur.

The boy kept yelling. His head bobbed under the water and up again. The waves were getting bigger, and the tide had come in. Murphy felt a knot of worry tighten in his stomach. He glanced back at the surf competition. Maybe he should stop the competition and call Boris and

the lifeguards. But Boris had said the boy was trying to fool them again. Surely Boris was right.

Murphy felt uneasy. He felt it deep down in his chest. His paws twitched. Maybe he would just take a walk along the beach and check if the boy was okay. He could be back before Aliikai had finished her turn.

Murphy trotted to the far end of the beach. The waves were different here. They didn't curl in a soft line but reared up in messy waves that thumped down on the sand. But where the boy was, the ocean was strangely flat. As Murphy watched, the boy seemed to be drifting farther and farther out, as if invisible hands were pulling him away from the shore.

Murphy knew the boy wasn't fooling around anymore. This boy was in deep, deep trouble.

This boy was in a rip current and being sucked out to sea.

Murphy didn't even think about it. He plunged into the water.

The first wave hit him, rolling him over, but he got up again and bounded farther into the water. He

remembered Rodrigo telling him to
keep his head down and let the waves
pass over him. He plunged through
the water, diving underneath each
mountainous wave. When he broke
past them, he could feel the rip current
take hold of him and pull him too. He
glanced back and watched the beach
disappear farther and farther away.

Keep calm, he told himself. *Don't
panic*. He had to find the boy. The
boy was underwater again. Murphy

couldn't see him, but he felt him with his paws. The boy held on to Murphy and pulled himself up again.

He took a huge gasp as his head burst above the water.

"Woof," Murphy barked. The boy's hand reached up and grasped the handles on Murphy's jacket. Together they spun in the rip current, heading out to sea.

Murphy knew it was hopeless to swim against the rip current. He had to swim out of it, parallel to the shoreline.

He could see people running along the beach toward them, Boris in front and all his friends not far behind.

Murphy turned and swam parallel to the beach. His legs ached. Water rushed up his nose and into his eyes, but he kept swimming until he felt the pull of the rip current weaken. Now all he had to do was swim to the shore. It was harder with the weight of the boy, and the waves seemed even bigger.

Murphy looked behind him to see a huge wave rise up. Everything slowed down. He thought of Rodrigo and how he had told Murphy not to fight

the ocean but to become part of
it. He didn't feel frightened
anymore.

"Hold on," Murphy woofed. He
pushed his paws in front of him and
prepared to bodysurf as the wave
curled over and raced them to the
shore.

"ARRRRRRROOOOOO!"
howled Murphy.

People were cheering along the
shoreline. Boris bounded in and
helped Murphy and the boy onto
the sand.

"Well done, young pup," woofed
Boris. "Well done."

The boy's mother rushed up and
held her son in her arms.

Murphy's friends crowded
around him. He was wet
and cold and plastered
in sand and seaweed.

"You're safe,
Murphy," cried Scruff.

"We thought we'd lost you," said Pip.

"You're our hero," said Rodrigo. Murphy smiled.

He smiled because he knew it didn't matter if he was a hero or not; his friends were there for him, and that meant more than anything in the world.

7

There was a buzz of excitement at
the puppy academy.

All the puppies filled the hall
and waited. It wasn't every day
that a world-famous celebrity visited
the academy. Murphy sat next to
Rodrigo and his friends and waited
for Boris of Bognor Regis.

"Here he comes," woofed Star.

The pups howled with excitement as
Boris walked into the hall.

"WELCOME, WELCOME, EVERYONE, TO THE FRIDAY AWARD CEREMONY," barked Professor Offenbach. "TODAY WE WELCOME BORIS OF BOGNOR REGIS TO PRESENT SOME VERY SPECIAL BADGES. WE ALSO SAY A VERY SAD FAREWELL TO OUR STUDENT FROM MEXICO, RODRIGO LOPEZ. I KNOW MANY OF YOU HAVE BECOME GREAT FRIENDS WITH HIM AND WILL KEEP IN CONTACT. WHO KNOWS, MAYBE SOME OF YOU WILL EVEN GET THE CHANCE TO VISIT HIM IN MEXICO ONE DAY."

Murphy looked at Rodrigo. "I don't want you to go," he said.

Rodrigo wagged his tail. "Amigo, come and visit me anytime. The surf is great in Mexico!"

"AND . . . ," continued Professor Offenbach, "I WOULD LIKE TO

CALL UP RODRIGO TO THE GIANT SAUSAGE PODIUM AND GIVE HIM A BAG OF SURFBOARD-SHAPED CRUNCHIE MUNCHIES IN CELEBRATION OF HIS FIFTH PLACE AT THE WORLD JUNIOR SURF DOG CHAMPIONSHIPS."

All the pups cheered and thumped their tails on the floor for Rodrigo, but none more loudly than Murphy.

"I WOULD NOW LIKE TO ASK BORIS TO PRESENT RODRIGO WITH THE SURF RESCUE BADGE."

Murphy watched Boris fix the

badge to Rodrigo's collar. He sighed.
He wished he'd been able to take the
test too.

"AND I WOULD LIKE TO CALL
UP MURPHY TO THE SAUSAGE
PODIUM, TOO, TO RECEIVE AN
AWARD."

Murphy didn't move.

"Go on," prodded Star.

"But I didn't take the test," said
Murphy.

Boris faced all the puppies. "Murphy made a few mistakes during his training. We all make mistakes. The important thing is to learn from them. I made the mistake of thinking a boy was fooling around again in the water. It was Murphy who trusted his instincts and did something incredibly brave. He risked his own life to save someone else's."

Silence fell across the hall.

Boris cleared his throat. "Because of his bravery in the face of extreme danger, I would like to present Murphy with the highest honor. . . ."

Murphy looked up to see Boris holding a gold medal in his paw.

"The Gold Medal for Gallantry."

All the puppies thumped their tails and howled.

Murphy's legs were shaking, but he made his way onto the podium. He looked into the Newfoundland's brave eyes. "You're my hero," Murphy whispered.

Boris of Bognor Regis placed the medal around Murphy's neck and smiled. "You're *my* hero too."

"One last swim in the river," woofed Rodrigo, jumping into the water with Pip and Scruff.

Murphy sat with Star on the riverbank.

"I'm going to miss him," said Murphy.

"Me too," said Star.

Major Bones sat down beside them. "Well done on your medal for gallantry," he said. "You were very brave indeed."

Murphy stared at his feet. "Anyone would have done the same," he said.

"Maybe," said Major Bones. "It was brave to swim out into those waves and save that boy. But courage comes in different forms. It was brave to get back up and go out into the waves when you were scared to try again. Not many would have given it another go."

"Rodrigo helped me with that,"

said Murphy. He sighed. "I feel so bad about being unfriendly to him when he arrived."

Star looked up at him. "You said you were sorry."

"Yes." Major Bones smiled. "And it can take even greater courage to say sorry and to admit that you were wrong."

Rodrigo splashed water at Murphy and Star. "Hey! Amigos! Aren't you coming in?"

"We're coming," yelled Star.

"WATCH OUT," woofed Murphy.

A huge brown blur whizzed through the air . . .

"ARRROOOOOOOOOOOO!"

Meet Whizz, a real-life water rescue dog!

Name
Whizz

Occupation
Water rescue and therapy dog

Likes
Company and cuddles

Hates
Hot weather (because he has a really thick double coat)

Whizz is lively and excited when leaping to the rescue, but as soon as he spends time with a sick child, he changes into a lovely, calm, cuddly friend.

Water Rescue Dog Facts

Leonbergers like Murphy and Newfoundlands like Boris make great water rescue dogs because of their size, stamina, and love of water!

Water rescue dogs sometimes have to tow boats.

DID YOU KNOW?

They also have to practice jumping off different types of boats.

The handle on a water rescue jacket has two uses: for the person being rescued to hold on to, and to help lift the dog back into a lifeboat.

DID YOU KNOW?

Leonbergers and Mexican Hairless dogs have flaps of skin between their toes, giving them webbed feet like a duck! This means they are excellent swimmers.

Another name for a Mexican Hairless dog like Rodrigo is Xoloitzcuintli (say "show-low-eats-queent-lee").

DID YOU KNOW?

Leonbergers have a double coat—long, oily hair covering soft, dense hair—which helps keep them warm in water.

About Murphy and his owner, Gill Lewis

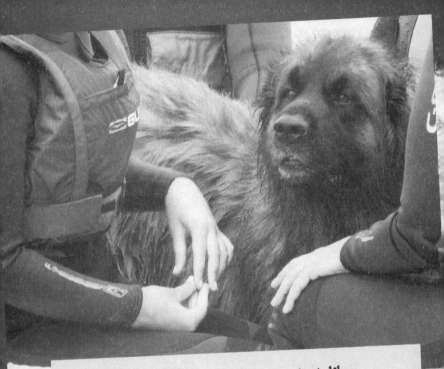

I'm **MURPHY**, a Leonberger just like Murphy in this book. He's named after me. I LOVE people and I LOVE water, which is why Leonbergers make such great water rescue dogs. Sometimes when I meet people, I get so excited that I forget just how big I am. But I'm a big dog with a big heart, and people seem to find me very huggable.

If you want, I'll come on all your adventures. I'll climb mountains and swim across rivers with you. I'm so strong, I'll even carry your picnic basket!

PUPPY PLEDGE

I promise to be honest, brave, and true and serve my fellow dogs and humans too.

In peril, I will be your guide, walking with you by your side.

I am your eyes, your ears, your nose, through wind and rain and sun and snow. I'll be with you until the very end, your wet-nosed, waggy-tailed best, best friend.